LIAM

D1519531

LIAM

TEXAS BOUDREAU BROTHERHOOD

By
KATHY IVAN

COPYRIGHT

Liam – Original Copyright © April 2022 by Kathy Ivan

Cover by Elizabeth Mackey of EMGRAPHICS

Release date: April 2022
Print Edition

All Rights Reserved

Liam – Texas Boudreau Brotherhood

Sometimes death isn't the end of the journey.

As a teen, Ruby Bright discovered the only way to prevent a massive tragedy befalling everyone she loved meant making a drastic choice—faking her death and disappearing.

Liam Boudreau grieved the girl he loved for ten long years, only to find out everything he believed was a lie. When the truth is exposed Liam finds himself face to face with a very-much-alive Ruby. The undeniable chemistry that once burned between them rages as strong as ever.

Now that he knows the truth, Liam must protect Ruby from the danger that's followed her Shiloh Springs. When the enemy strikes, can they count on each other to overcome the obstacles which could set them both free and fight for the love they deserve?

BOOKS BY KATHY IVAN

www.kathyivan.com/books.html

TEXAS BOUDREAU BROTHERHOOD
Rafe

Antonio

Brody

Ridge

Lucas

Heath

Shiloh

Chance

Derrick

Dane

Liam

Brian (coming soon)

Texas Boudreau Brotherhood Series Box Set Books 1-3

NEW ORLEANS CONNECTION SERIES
Desperate Choices

Connor's Gamble

Relentless Pursuit

Ultimate Betrayal

Keeping Secrets

Sex, Lies and Apple Pies

Deadly Justice

Wicked Obsession

Hidden Agenda

Spies Like Us

Fatal Intentions

New Orleans Connection Series Box Set: Books 1-3
New Orleans Connection Series Box Set: Books 4-7

CAJUN CONNECTION SERIES
Saving Sarah
Saving Savannah
Saving Stephanie
Guarding Gabi

LOVIN' LAS VEGAS SERIES
It Happened in Vegas
Crazy Vegas Love
Marriage, Vegas Style
A Virgin in Vegas
Vegas, Baby!
Yours For the Holidays
Match Made in Vegas
One Night in Vegas
Last Chance in Vegas
Lovin' Las Vegas (box set books 1-3)

OTHER BOOKS BY KATHY IVAN
Second Chances (Destiny's Desire Book #1)
Losing Cassie (Destiny's Desire Book #2)

Dear Reader,

Welcome to Shiloh Springs, Texas! Don't you just love a small Texas town, where the people are neighborly, the gossip plentiful, and the heroes are ...well, heroic, not to mention easy on the eyes! I love everything about Texas, which I why I've made the great state my home for over thirty years. There's no other place like it. From the delicious Tex-Mex food and downhome barbecue, the majestic scenery, and friendly atmosphere, the people and places of the Lone Star state are as unique and colorful as you'll find anywhere.

The Texas Boudreau Brotherhood series centers around a group of foster brothers, men who would have ended up in the system if not for Douglas and Patricia Boudreau. Instead of being hardened by life and circumstances beyond their control, they found a family who loved and accepted them, and gave them a place to call home. Sometimes brotherhood is more than sharing the same DNA.

If you've read my other romantic suspense books (the New Orleans Connection series and Cajun Connection series), you'll be familiar with the Boudreau name. Turns out there are a whole lot of Boudreaus out there, just itching to have their stories told. (Douglas is the brother of Gator Boudreau, patriarch of the New Orleans branch of the Boudreau family.) And keep your eyes peeled, because you might see a few more Boudreaus popping up around Shiloh Springs, because Douglas and Gator have another brother— Hank "The Tank" Boudreau.

So, sit back and relax. The pace of small-living might be

less hectic than the big city, but small towns hold secrets, excitement, and heroes to ride to the rescue. And who doesn't love a Texas cowboy?

Kathy Ivan

EDITORIAL REVIEWS

"Kathy Ivan's books are addictive, you can't read just one."

—Susan Stoker, NYT Bestselling Author

"Kathy Ivan's books give you everything you're looking for and so much more."

—Geri Foster, USA Today and NYT Bestselling Author of the Falcon Securities Series

"In Shiloh Springs, Kathy Ivan has crafted warm, engaging characters that will steal your heart and a mystery that will keep you reading to the very last page."

—Barb Han, *USA TODAY* and Publisher's Weekly Bestselling Author

"This is the first I have read from Kathy Ivan and it won't be the last."

—Night Owl Reviews

"I highly recommend Desperate Choices. Readers can't go wrong here!"

—Melissa, Joyfully Reviewed

"I loved how the author wove a very intricate storyline with plenty of intriguing details that led to the final reveal…"

—Night Owl Reviews

Desperate Choices—Winner 2012 International Digital Award—Suspense

Desperate Choices—Best of Romance 2011 –Joyfully Reviewed

DEDICATIONS AND ACKNOWLEDGEMENTS

To my sister, Mary Sullivan, for her unwavering belief that I write good stories. She is always there, helping me, encouraging me, and doing whatever it takes to help me get the writing done. Trust me, if she wasn't there prodding me, the books might never get finished. And I always dedicate books to my mother, Betty Sullivan. Her love of reading and sharing her love for books, no matter the genre, set me on the path to storytelling. She instilled in me the joy of reading and a love of romance. A special shout out to all the readers, who keep me going. Knowing that you enjoy my books and keep asking for more, there's no greater feeling in the world.

More about Kathy and her books can be found at

WEBSITE:
www.kathyivan.com

Follow Kathy on Facebook at
facebook.com/kathyivanauthor

Follow Kathy on Twitter at
twitter.com/@kathyivan

Follow Kathy at BookBub
bookbub.com/profile/kathy-ivan

NEWSLETTER SIGN UP

Don't want to miss any new books, contests, and free stuff? Sign up to get my newsletter. I promise not to spam you, and only send out notifications/e-mails whenever there's a new release or contest/giveaway. Follow the link and join today!

LIAM

CHAPTER ONE

L IAM BOUDREAU RAN his fingertip across the face in the worn photograph for the hundredth time since Brian handed it to him days earlier. The guy seemed to turn up like a bad penny every time a threat to a Boudreau reared its ugly head. He'd helped uncover the truth about the hit on Dane's life. He'd even kidnapped Tina, Chance's fiancée, to keep her safe from a ruthless killer. Way to make an impression.

But the biggest bombshell he'd dropped as far as Liam was concerned? Giving him false hope. It was cruel, a punch-to-the-gut blow that turned his world on its head. Every time he looked at the smiling face in the photograph, the brilliant blue eyes of the woman so happy and vibrant, his gut knotted. The grief he'd held close for so many years weighed him down like a boulder atop his shoulders. The desolation and loss he endured—still did—threatened to consume him until nothing remained but a husk of what he'd been. It would hardly differ from what he felt now, because he'd been little more than a zombie moving through life since he'd lost her.

In this picture, Ruby looked older than the seventeen-year-old girl he remembered. Whoever took the pic hadn't managed to capture the *joie de verve*, the spark he always caught in her gaze when she smiled at him. This Ruby, standing beside a nondescript white four-door sedan in an equally nondescript strip mall parking lot, was his Ruby—yet not. The long blonde hair he'd loved running his fingers through was shorter now, barely reaching the tops of her shoulders. It was several shades darker, too. When he'd known her, the color had been lighter, an almost white-blonde. Had she taken to coloring it, or had it darkened naturally over the missing years?

Her sparkling blue eyes, always filled with love and laughter, looked more haunted than happy. The thin frame she'd had as a teen had filled out, giving her an hourglass figure with curves in all the right places. This woman was no longer a teenager with hopes and dreams ahead of her. No, this was a world-weary woman who seemed to have the weight of the world on her shoulders.

It was Ruby; he didn't doubt that for an instant. Nobody made his heartbeat race or caused the breath to catch in the back of his throat the way she did. He'd never forgotten the first time he'd seen her, felt the instant connection when he'd plowed into her in the hallway at the Shiloh Springs Elementary School. From that moment, his world seemed to right itself on its axis, and he'd known why he'd ended up in this small town.

He flipped over the photo and read the two words printed on the back. Words that managed to shake him to his foundation.

She's alive.

It was impossible. He'd been there when the paramedics worked on her, struggled to keep her breathing, to keep her heart beating. He'd followed the ambulance to the hospital, the never-ending sound of the wailing sirens echoing its eerie cry. Watched as the gurney swept past him into the emergency room.

Heard the lone solitary beep as the heart monitor flat-lined.

He'd buried her along with his heart that cold, dreary Friday afternoon and hadn't truly felt alive a day since. Every day since losing Ruby, he'd merely gone through the motions because he knew his family, the people Liam loved more than anything, needed to believe he could go on without the other half of his soul. Then, with two seemingly insignificant words, his entire world tilted, throwing his whole being into a tailspin.

After dropping his bombshell, Brian took off before Liam got a chance to demand answers, disappearing like a phantom in the mist. If he got his hands on the dude, he'd— shoot, he'd probably do nothing because it would upset his momma.

I really hate that guy.

"Hey, boss, you got a second? Harry's got questions

about the changes in the layout, and he needs you to sign off before the guys start."

"Be right there."

Liam slid the picture inside his wallet and into his back pocket. He didn't have time to deal with imaginary ghosts from the past. Instead, he had a job to do and a crew to supervise. Boudreau Construction might be his dad's pride and joy, but Liam had worked for the family's company for years, gaining the trust and respect of all the members of his crews. Now, he was second in command only to his father, who was slowly turning over more responsibility to Liam, and was easing his way closer to completely turning over the reins of the company. Of course, it wouldn't be anytime soon—and that was fine with Liam. He loved working with his father—but he felt a sense of pride and accomplishment when he looked at what he'd helped build.

After dealing with the questions about the condos' revised layout and changes to the blueprints, he pulled out his phone and dialed his mother's number. None of his brothers seemed to have a way to contact Brian, which drove Liam insane. How did the man keep popping up, disrupting their lives, and then go along his merry way without leaving a phone number or an e-mail? He knew his momma had Brian's number; he'd stated as much the last time Liam saw the man, right before he'd tossed the envelope containing Ruby's photo into his lap and blown out of town like a bloody phantom.

"Good morning, honey. Tell me you made your dad grab something to eat this morning. He snuck away before breakfast."

Liam chuckled at his mother's concern. True to form, she always ensured everybody was okay, like a mother hen with all her baby chicks. Of course, part of that concern was making sure they had full bellies.

"Hi, Momma. Yes, we stopped and picked up breakfast sandwiches, juice, and coffee from Daisy's on the way to the site. He's stuffed full and in the trailer dealing with paperwork."

"Which means he's in a foul mood. He'd much rather be out working with the crew, getting his hands dirty. Anyway, what can I do for you?"

Liam heard the engine's hum, the barely-there music playing on the radio through the phone's speaker. Momma must be on the way to one of her listings. As one of the most prestigious real estate agents in Central Texas, she was a ball of fire when dealing with her clients and showing properties. He didn't worry about her being out and about, at least not much. Her company remained one of the prestigious real estate companies in Central Texas. Patricia Boudreau tended to be far too trusting, and he occasionally wondered if some unscrupulous idiot might try to take advantage of her. Then he remembered his mother had ten able-bodied sons and one take-no-prisoners husband, and the worry faded.

"Do you have a way of contacting Brian? Phone number,

maybe?"

"Why?" Despite the slowly drawn-out word, he heard the underlying edge of caution in her voice.

"Don't worry, Momma; he's not in trouble." *Yet.* "I need to clarify something he mentioned when he was here."

"You sure? Because you've been on edge for the last couple of days. Don't deny it. I'm your mother, and I notice everything. Especially when my son's withdrawing, distancing from the rest of the family. I promised your dad I'd stay out of it, give you a chance to come to us. But if you're looking for Brian…"

Great, she'd been talking to his father about him. That wasn't good. It did explain the sideways glances his dad had been shooting his way the past couple of days. Nope, he changed his mind. He couldn't open her up to the same heartache he'd gone through the past few days. Ruby had been like a part of the family to her. Watching his momma grieve her again when the truth came out, and they found out this was all an elaborate ruse, or worse, an extortion attempt to grab cash from his family? It would never be worth the price if it broke her heart again. Besides, until he had proof, everything was simple speculation. Smoke and mirrors meant to disorient and befuddle the mind.

Too bad it's working.

Could he let it go? The not knowing, the constant niggling in the back of his head wondering if Ruby was still alive? Was somebody playing a huge cosmic joke on him just to watch him go insane? Even if it opened him up for untold misery, he couldn't let it go. He had to know the truth.

"Momma, don't worry. You know what, never mind. I don't need to talk to Brian. It's not important."

"Liam Boudreau, who do you think you're talking to? You might lie to yourself, but you can't get away with lying to me. Tell me what's wrong, because if you don't, I'm gonna call Brian myself and find out what's going on. And you know I'll do it."

Liam sighed, knowing he'd just unleashed a whole new set of problems. There wouldn't be any keeping Momma out of things now. If he didn't head her off, she'd pull in Dad and all his brothers, which was the last thing he needed. He'd tell them eventually because if Ruby was alive somewhere and needed help, he'd do whatever it took to find her, bring her back home.

"It's probably nothing. Brian mentioned something to me when he was here, and I need to get a little more information before I decide what to do about it."

"Uh-huh. Not good enough, kiddo. You always do this. Minimize and evade giving a straightforward answer. You'll hem and haw around the issue without actually saying anything. Either tell me what's wrong or I'll call your father, and you can explain to him why you're evading answering my question. I'd head straight to your job site if I were close enough, but I'm in the opposite direction. I can always sic your dad on you, son. He'll get the answers I want, and you know I'll do it in a heartbeat."

She'd do it too, he knew.

"When Brian was here, he gave me something. A photograph. All I want is his number so I can call and ask him why he gave me that picture."

Would she buy it?

"A picture of what?"

Guess not.

He sighed. "Ruby."

His mother's quickly indrawn breath was audible through the phone. Closing his eyes, he squeezed the bridge of his nose between his finger and thumb, wishing he'd kept his mouth shut. This was precisely why he hadn't wanted to pull her into this mess, open old wounds. One more strike against Brian.

"Why would Brian give you a photo of Ruby? How does he even know about her?"

"Precisely what I plan to ask him, Momma."

"Tell me about this picture. It must be significant or Brian wouldn't have given it to you. He didn't live with us when you were with Ruby, but he must know how important she was to you. To all of us." There was a pause before she added, "I miss her, too."

"I know. I need to question Brian without dragging everybody else into this."

"This what? Giving you an old photo of your former girlfriend is cruel, and I can't see Brian deliberately hurting you. Son, this picture obviously has you shook, so just tell me."

"I can't convince you to let this go, and just give me Brian's number, can I?" Her chuckle was all the answer he needed. "Momma, the picture of Ruby...it isn't an old photo. So, unless Brian is a master of Photoshop and really wants to stick it to me, it's new, or at least taken within the last year or two."

There was a long pause before his mother's voice came through the phone again, and he could practically feel the chill radiating off her words.

"That's not funny, Liam."

"Exactly. Brian tossed me an envelope with Ruby's photo in it with 'she's alive' written on the back, a cryptic message to call him if I wanted to know more, and then ghosted. Believe me, when I get hold of his sorry—"

"I want to see it," she interrupted, her voice brooking no-nonsense.

Liam took a deep breath, exhaling slowly. This was precisely why he'd tried to keep his mother out of things until he had more information. She'd adored Ruby, and the feeling had been mutual. Ruby thought his momma was the next best thing to heaven since she'd lost her own mother when she was a kid. Being raised by a single dad, he'd done the best he could with Ruby. Still, nobody could make you feel cherished as a mother did, and Patricia Boudreau had showered Ruby with so much affection, claiming she was practically family.

"Momma, let me talk to Brian." *Assuming the big jerk doesn't ditch my call.* "Try and get some answers from him. I'll meet you at the Big House tonight when I drop Dad home. I'll bring the picture with me. Good enough?"

"For now."

"You'll give me Brian's number?"

"Hang on a second." The call was put on hold, and he tilted his head back, staring at the sky. The vivid blue was crystal clear, nary a cloud obscuring any of the brilliant color. It reminded him of Ruby's eyes. He couldn't count the number of times he'd found himself lost in them, the color sometimes deepening with her emotions, but the hues of blue were as unique as the girl herself.

"Liam?"

"I'm here, Momma."

She rattled off a number, spitting out the digits, her voice harsh and angry. Uh oh, Momma Bear was definitely peeved. He winced, guilty he'd brought those feelings to the forefront. If he'd been able to get in touch with Brian any other way, he'd have taken it, kept his mother from going through the familiar anguish he'd dealt with for the past couple of days.

"Thanks. I'll let you know what Brian says."

"If he gives you any guff, let me know. I'll straighten him out on exactly how Boudreaus treat one another."

He bit back the retort that Brian wasn't a Boudreau. Ever

since the other man showed up in Shiloh Springs, his mother had developed an almost unhealthy affection for him. If he found out Brian was running some scam or playing his mother for a fool, FBI agent or not, he'd teach the man a lesson in what dealing with the Boudreau clan truly meant. And he'd have no problem pulling his brothers in to assist.

Liam also noted her not-so-subtle reminder. Family was everything and didn't keep secrets. His mother let him know he'd have some penance of his own upcoming in her unique way.

"See you tonight, Momma. Love you."

"I love you too, Liam. Tell your daddy I'll call him later."

Liam was smart enough to read between the lines of his mother's coolly-delivered statement. He'd better tell his dad what was happening, or she would.

Message received.

Disconnecting the call, he picked up the roll of blueprints before shoving his phone in his back pocket, then pulled it out again and stared at the black screen. He'd input the number as his mother gave it to him, so he didn't have an excuse not to call Brian and get the whole unvarnished truth about Ruby. Yet he couldn't bring himself to hit dial.

What if it was all a lie? An elaborate ruse to rip his heart open and stomp on the raw pieces? He shook his head, denying the impromptu thought. It couldn't be because nobody hated him enough to wreak that kind of devastation on his soul. Without a good reason, he doubted even *Brian the Jerk* would pull something heinous enough to alienate himself from the rest of the Boudreaus, especially his mother. He'd worked too hard to worm his way back into her good graces.

He tossed the blueprints back onto the tabletop, and taking a deep breath hit dial.

CHAPTER TWO

RUBY BRIGHT LOOPED an arm around the teen's shoulder and gave a gentle squeeze. Katie had arrived at their shelter two nights previous, brought in by one of Haven of Hope's benefactors. She called him a benefactor, though she didn't know much about him. Gage Newsome showed up out of the blue, usually with a homeless kid in tow and a pocketful of cash to cover expenses. It hadn't taken her long to figure out he liked playing the hero, silently helping teens and young adults who weren't hardened by life on the streets or those who'd run away and needed a safe place to rest and a shoulder to cry on. All without wanting any credit and especially no publicity. He was like a ghost, moving silently through the night, often disappearing without uttering a single goodbye.

Dealing with kids desperate for help, that's where Ruby entered the picture. She and her partner, Lucy Felton, ran the small halfway house on a shoestring budget. Funds were always short, and need far exceeded what they could provide, but they did their best. Wichita Falls, Texas, could be scary if you didn't have a roof over your head or food in your belly.

It was a sad fact of life predators stalked the streets and were everywhere, even in smaller towns. Unfortunately, she'd witnessed firsthand that big cities weren't the only places where evil existed.

"Ms. Ruby, how long can I stay here before I have to leave?" Katie's voice quivered, barely above a whisper, and Ruby heard the quiet desolation beneath the young girl's simple question. She shook off the memories of having voiced the same question years before.

Don't think about that now. Focus on the present. Katie needs love and somebody she can trust. Get your head in the game.

"You can stay as long as you want, hon."

"But—"

"No buts. This is a safe place. You're welcome to stay as long as you want, Katie. How about we put your stuff in your room and grab some dinner? Lucy made enchiladas. They are delicious. I wish I could cook half as good as she does. Me? I can barely boil water. I'm banned from the kitchen."

Ruby watched Katie's lips curl upward in a shy smile. "I like to cook. Well, I like to bake."

"Girl, if you tell Lucy that, she'll have you in the kitchen so fast your feet won't hit the floor. She has a raging sweet tooth but never has the time to bake. We buy all our baked goods from the grocery store, but they don't taste the same as homemade."

Ruby stopped in front of a closed door halfway down the hallway. It was their last open room for the night and held two sets of bunk beds. Unfortunately, two were occupied, and with Katie moving in, that left only one free bed, and they were full up, which was good and bad. Good that they provided a safe place for those in need. Bad because so many of them needed a place like Haven of Hope at all.

Opening the door, she gestured toward the bunks on the left. "You can take the top or bottom bunk over there. Why don't you get settled in and meet me in the kitchen in a few minutes?"

Katie took a hesitant step through the open door and spun toward Ruby, wrapping her arms around her and squeezing tight. Ruby's arms came up, and she hugged Katie back, knowing the teen desperately craved affection and acceptance. She'd been quiet the day before and managed to sneak away in the early morning hours without a word. Ruby didn't know where she'd been throughout the day, though she had a good idea. And it broke her heart. Then, just before dark, Katie showed up outside their house, stood before the wrought iron fence, and stared up at the two-story house, indecision on her face. Her shoulders were stooped like she wanted to appear smaller—maybe invisible. Ruby made her way down the front porch steps and brought her inside.

Katie had taken the first step by showing up again. It was a start, significant and hopeful. Better than the opposite as far as Ruby was concerned. Far too many of the kids who came through their doors disappeared, never to be heard from again. The ones who remained, though—they were the ones who grabbed her by the heart because they had a chance. It might be a small, almost-impossible-to-make-it shot, but staying meant they were willing to take the first step.

Like Liam had.

Ruby drew in a ragged breath when she thought about the boy she'd fallen head over heels in love with when she'd been a naïve teenager, full of giddy dreams of happily ever after.

Don't go there, Ruby. You can't ever go back.

Glancing at the clock over the stove, she nearly panicked. She was supposed to meet Gage at the diner. Even if she left now, she was going to be late.

"Lucy, I've gotta run. Can you keep an eye on things?"

"No problem. Katie getting settled in?"

"Yes. She'll be down in a few minutes. She needs to be treated with kid gloves tonight. I think she's had a rough day. I want to stay, but if I don't meet Gage..."

"Go. We need that donation. Don't worry about a thing; I've got you covered."

Pulling in a deep breath, Ruby grabbed her purse and headed for her car. Something told her it was going to be a long night.

LIAM PULLED HIS pickup into the truck stop's parking lot and climbed out. He looked around at the line of eighteen-wheelers waiting to gas up, others parked in the oversized lot, the drivers probably inside the rundown-appearing diner. He grimaced. He wasn't looking forward to this meeting. Brian the Jerk, as he would always be known to Liam, had picked the place and time. Trust him to choose an out-of-the-way greasy spoon hundreds of miles from Shiloh Springs. He probably did it on purpose, trying to get a rise out of him.

Congratulations, dude, it's working.

It took nearly five hours to drive the three hundred plus miles from Shiloh Springs to this backwater spot Brian chose. When he'd answered Liam's call earlier, he'd been far too cagey about his responses, although Brian swore he'd give him the answers he needed. But he was in the middle of something important, which Liam took to mean his work with the FBI. So, he gave him the address for the truck stop and hung up.

So here he was, three hundred miles from home, all because he couldn't stand not knowing the truth about Ruby. Off to his right, he spotted a couple of women he felt confident weren't professional truck drivers, although they were definitely professionals. Shaking his head, he walked the short distance to the diner and yanked open the door. Immediately, he was met with the scent of oily fried food, the overwhelming smell of overused grease permeating the air. The underlying aroma of pepper gravy was the next fragrance to tickle his senses. He'd eaten in enough truck stops and diners with the work crews to know everything got drowned in gravy, especially if it had been deep-fried first.

He spotted Brian in a booth near the back and headed over, sliding into the seat across from him. There were dark circles beneath Brian's eyes, and he looked like he'd slept in his clothes. Chances were good he probably had, given how he'd sounded earlier when Liam had called.

"Why'd I have to drive almost five hours for something you could've told me over the phone?"

"Hello to you, too." When the waitress glanced their way, Brian raised a hand, pointed to his coffee cup, and lifted two fingers. "Sorry to inconvenience you, but I'm in the middle of something and couldn't make it to Shiloh Springs today. You didn't sound like you were willing to wait for answers, so this was the next best option."

When the waitress walked up, coffee pot in hand, he stopped talking. She topped off his cup and poured one for Liam. Smiling his thanks, he picked it up, took a sip, and grimaced at the strong, bitter brew. Definitely truck-stop coffee, extra strong to keep the drivers on their toes and wide awake for the next leg of their trip.

"Tell me what you know."

Brian sighed before gently placing his coffee cup on the tabletop, his meaty fist wrapped around it. His bloodshot eyes and the two-day-old scruff on his face told their own story. Liam almost felt sorry for him.

Almost.

"You know about my keeping tabs on your family and everything in Shiloh Springs that affects them." It was more a statement than a question.

Liam nodded. He knew about Brian's not-so-secret obsession with the Boudreaus. Momma dragged that fact out of him when he'd first showed back up at the Big House during the whole debacle with Tina's kidnapping. Sure, he'd done it to keep her alive, but Liam still didn't trust Brian. Too many unanswered questions.

Brian was one of the boys who'd lived at the ranch for a few months. He didn't personally remember him because he'd been gone when Liam moved to Shiloh Springs and became a member of the Boudreau clan. He didn't have many details about why Brian hadn't lasted with his family, though he admitted to a certain curiosity.

Maybe he should have Shiloh or Ridge do a deep dive into Brian's background. He gave a self-deprecating laugh. Who was he kidding? They probably already had a file a foot thick on the man, starting from the moment he'd reappeared in their lives. Things had been a little crazy the past couple of months, so Brian hadn't exactly been the big topic of discussion. He made a mental note to call his brothers sooner rather than later.

"I can't give you details about the case I'm currently

working on, but I've been in Wichita Falls for a while. I know another agent, working a completely different case, totally unrelated."

Liam kept silent, though it took an effort. He wished Brian would get to the point—tell him about Ruby. That's why he was here, after all. He picked up his coffee, downing a big swallow, and felt the heat pervade him. The feeling something big was coming teased at the back of his mind, and he felt antsy. Could it have something to do with whatever Brian was about to tell him? He bit back the urge to reach across and shake the dude because he needed to know what happened to Ruby and, more importantly, where was she now?

"I honestly wasn't paying much attention to Jaxon, the FBI agent I talked about. Brother loves to hear himself talk. But I took notice when he mentioned a name I recognized."

"Who?"

Brian straightened from his slouch, his gaze fixed on the diner's front door. Liam got an itch between his shoulder blades, that inner instinct he got when something was about to happen. It was a feeling he paid attention to because it has saved his backside on more than one occasion.

"Speak of the devil." He shook his head with Liam started to turn toward the door. "No, don't. It's been a long time, but he might recognize you."

"Who might recognize me?" Anger simmered right beneath the surface because he was done. Done playing games with Brian and feeling like he'd been led around by his nose, he disregarded Brian's low-voiced protest. Shifting on the booth's seat, he glanced toward the door. A tall, dark-haired stranger strode through and slid onto one of the vinyl-covered stools at the counter.

"I don't know who he is." Liam turned toward Brian with a frown. "Why would he recognize me?"

"Since you've already looked at him, think for a minute. He's older, a lot taller and broader than he used to be."

Liam glanced toward the stranger again, doing a more thorough study. Maybe late twenties or early thirties, he was broad across the shoulders like he worked out. He had dark hair and what looked like from this distance dark eyes, though he hadn't caught more than a passing glance at them. His face was covered with a short-cropped beard. He couldn't say he recognized him, although there was some-thing about the way he sat, kind of hunched over, the tilt of his head slightly to the left, with both hands wrapped around his coffee that felt familiar. Reminded him of—

"Gage? Is that Gage?"

Brian nodded. "He's been showing up in Wichita Falls on and off for the last year or so. Doesn't seem to have a local address, at least not one Jaxon found."

"Your interest in him is because he was at the Big House for a while?"

"In the beginning, yeah." Brian's steady gaze bored into him like he was trying to pass along a message without spitting out the words. Too bad Liam didn't speak subtle. Direct and to the point was more his style.

"Whatever you know, just spit it out. I'm tired, it's been a bloody long day, and you still haven't told me what you know about Ruby."

"That's just it, Boudreau. He's the thread I followed and found your Ruby. According to Jaxson, Gage Newsome has met with Ruby once a month for the past fourteen months."

"And he didn't bother to let us know she was alive? He's a dead man."

Liam started sliding across the booth's seat, intent on getting to the man who'd know about Ruby and kept the information secret. Gage had lived at the Boudreau ranch and knew how he felt about Ruby. Gage was one of the lost boys who'd stuck around the ranch for almost a year before he left. Social workers showed up out of the blue one day, and he'd been gone without explanation or notice. He remembered his momma crying for days afterward, another strike against the man about to get his butt kicked.

Brian's huge foot blocked him from exiting the booth. "Don't."

"Move."

"You can't confront him. Not yet."

Liam huffed out a ragged breath and slapped his hand against the tabletop. "Why not?"

Brian nodded toward the diner's door. "That's why."

Everything around Liam blurred, and time slowed when

he saw Ruby walk through the door. Time seemed to stop until the only sound he heard was the rapid thudding of his heartbeat. She was beautiful. Even under the harsh fluorescent lights, she glowed with an inner loveliness time hadn't dimmed.

The picture he'd been studying for the past few days didn't do her justice. It hadn't captured how her hair curved to frame her face or the way her eyes sparkled with an inner joy that couldn't be disguised. When she saw Gage, her lips curled upward in a smile that felt like a kick to his gut. She hadn't looked around, hadn't noticed anybody but Gage sitting at the diner's counter.

"You knew she'd be here?" He bit out the words, heard the anger and bitterness coloring them, and didn't care. The reunion he'd pictured, where she'd run to him, shattered into a million tiny pieces. She wasn't looking at him, wasn't smiling to let him know she'd missed him. Her sole focus was on Gage, the man who was about to feel Liam's fist knocking out all those pearly whites he flashed at Ruby.

"Jaxon said he followed Gage here. Not sure why he did because Gage isn't the target of his investigation, not directly, but he said something about the guy felt off, so he trusted his gut and tailed him. He's met with Ruby at this truck stop three times that he knows of."

He couldn't take his eyes off her. Felt the mule kick to the side of his head when she slid onto the seat beside Gage and leaned in to hug him. He fisted his hands, fighting the urge to jump from the booth and rip Gage's head off.

"Either get a grip, Liam, or I'll haul you out the back. You can't attack him in the middle of the place with all these witnesses. Play it cool because this is probably the only chance you'll get to see your gal. She's skittish, and if she's spooked, she's gonna bolt."

"What's with all the horse references? She's not a filly being broken to bit."

"No," Brian admitted, "but she needs to be treated with kid gloves because there's something she's hiding, and if she heads for the hills, we may never find her again. I can tell you she isn't using her real name. She still goes by Ruby, but the last name has changed at least four times that I could track. Probably a heck of a lot more. Do you want to lose her before you've even talked?"

Liam closed his eyes and counted to ten, something his dad always made him do when he'd been on the verge of losing his cool. He'd been a hot-tempered adolescent and spent more than his fair share of time in the barn with his dad, learning to control his anger issues. Now he felt like he was back to being that hot-headed kid who hit first and didn't bother asking questions.

He held up a hand, letting Brian know he'd reined in his impetuous need to race across the diner and tear Gage's head off his shoulders, though it still felt like a good idea. He could always hold that as option B.

"I'm not getting a romantic vibe from those two."

Liam jerked his head around and glared at Brian. "What?"

"Dude, be a little more subtle, will ya? If you don't want them to notice you, stop making it so bloody obvious you're watching them. Shooting daggers at Gage isn't doing a bit of good." Brian nodded toward Gage and Ruby. "Other than giving him a friendly hug when she sat down, she hasn't leaned toward him. He hasn't touched her hand or given any indication he's more than a friend. They're talking, but I'm not getting any body language that's screaming couple." Brian silently rapped his knuckles against the tabletop. "And stop swiveling around and staring. You are making it obvious you're interested in their every move. Undercover work isn't in your genes."

"No, I leave that to my brothers."

Brian grinned. "Yeah, they're good. I know they've run traces on me. Shiloh even has Destiny digging. She's good, but I've got safeguards that even she hasn't cracked."

"Yet," Liam taunted.

Liam studied the man across from him, noting the deep lines on his forehead and the ones bracketing his mouth. If he had to guess, he'd think Brian led a hard life. He found himself wishing Brian had stayed at the Boudreau ranch. On the plus side, it looked like he'd turned out okay, since he was working for the good guys. His momma trusted him, and that was good enough for Liam. *For now.*

"Do not turn around. Gage just passed Ruby an envelope, and it looks thick. Probably cash. Dude, I said don't turn around. It's like I'm dealing with a three-year-old."

Liam shot him his middle finger and barely refrained from sliding from the booth. Brian was right; the envelope Ruby slid into her purse was precisely the right size to hold a chunk of money. The big question was, why would Gage give Ruby money?

She spent a few minutes talking with Gage and sipping on a glass of iced tea. Brian was right, they didn't give off any vibe that they were a couple. Friends maybe, definitely more than simple acquaintances, but no spark between the two.

Good.

Watching her move reinforced how much he'd missed her. He knew the anger would come rushing back. Being a cuckold wasn't a good feeling, but right now, the simple fact his Ruby still breathed the same air, and sat less than a hundred feet away, made a burgeoning hope spring up inside his chest.

Another minute passed, and then two. Brian sat quietly. He appreciated the other man giving him a few minutes because right now, up was down, and down was up. Trying to wrap his head around what his eyes showed him still didn't seem real: a walking, talking miracle that had sprung to life in front of him.

He shifted in his chair when Gage stood and dropped a soft kiss against the top of Ruby's head. What was that son of a gun up to? With a swagger like he owned the place, Gage strode out of the diner. Ruby stayed seated, finishing her tea. She dropped a few ones onto the counter and stood and swung her bag over her shoulder, heading for the door.

"Hate to cut things short, Brian, but I've gotta run."

"Gonna chase the pretty girl, Liam? I get it. You need anything, you've got my number."

"Thanks, man. I mean that. If you hadn't given me that picture—"

"Don't. You'd have done the same for me. Now get out of here and get the girl. But, dude, be careful. Still waters run deep with that gal. Watch your back."

Without another word, Liam followed Ruby, carefully staying hidden out of sight. He watched her head toward a four-door sedan, a nondescript white color, like hundreds of others. Nothing about it stood out, except that it had to be at least ten, maybe twelve years old. There were a few dents and dings, and a pretty good chunk of the trunk had rust spots, but it must run because it got her here.

He heard the beep-beep of the car unlocking and sped up, jogging to keep up with Ruby. Patience was the key to getting what he needed. Just a few more steps.

Ruby slid behind the wheel, and Liam knew he had to make his move. It was now or never.

Yanking the front passenger door open, he slid onto the seat and heard her sharp gasp. Now he had her right where he wanted her.

"Hello, Ruby."

CHAPTER THREE

RUBY'S HEARTBEAT RACED fast enough she felt like she'd pass out. She couldn't believe her eyes because the last person she expected to slide onto the car seat beside her was Liam Boudreau. The man she'd left behind, even when it had broken her heart. He couldn't be here—it was impossible. Yet she knew she wasn't dreaming. The anger radiating from him was real, pulsing with an unleashed energy, waiting to spring forth.

"Liam? I…what are you doing here?"

"I think the better question is, why did you never tell me you were alive?"

"I couldn't."

She studied him, her gaze roaming over every inch of his face. So much had changed over the years they'd been apart. He'd matured from the young boy she'd fallen madly in love with into a handsome man. All the youthful cuteness which held such promise of developing into a good-looking man far exceeded anything she could have imagined. The soft cheeks and jawline of the teenage boy had morphed into adult features, and though he was older, she would have recognized him anywhere, no matter how much time had passed. No, he wasn't model perfect. Nevertheless, his face held character. His dark hair curling along the top of his collar to the straight blade of his nose. There was an intensity and sharpness that made him all male.

His body had changed too. Before, he'd been all gangly arms and legs, growing so fast he'd been a bit clumsy. Now he was tall and lean with a predatory grace which should have frightened her—yet she wasn't afraid. She could never be scared of Liam. Muscular shoulders and arms were encased in a flannel shirt, the buttons straining against a chest she itched to run her hands across, to feel the lines and curves. To relearn every inch of him, trace the changes from boy to man.

But the Liam seated beside her wasn't the same boy she knew. He was older, harder, without a hint of the fun-loving Boudreau son she'd adored. Emotions slammed into her, racing one after the next, and she nearly drowned under the weight of those emotions. She remembered how much she'd missed him every day they'd been apart. He'd been the love of her life. Her soulmate. Every thought, every plan they discussed had been so they could be together forever. They'd planned their whole life, starting after graduation. Her world had been perfect—until it wasn't.

"You couldn't tell me you were alive? Couldn't take two minutes out of your hectic schedule to pick up a phone and say, 'Hey, Liam, guess what? They didn't pronounce me dead in the emergency room, it was a huge mistake. That wasn't me in the casket you buried. I'm alive, but I can't see you anymore. Oops, my bad.'"

She hid the flinch his words caused, like an invisible blow, knowing she deserved every one of his accusations. It didn't matter there'd been a good excuse not to contact him. He'd needed to believe she died. Everyone did.

"Liam, I can't explain. I'm sorry."

"Can't or won't?"

She kept her gaze lowered, refusing to mee his intent stare. "Can't, won't, it doesn't matter. You need to leave." Finally raising her head, she met his gaze, almost flinching under the anger simmering beneath the surface. "Have you told anybody? About me being alive?"

"Just Momma."

Tears prickled behind her eyelids when he mentioned his mother. Ms. Patti had been a second mother to her. Her own abandoned her when she was barely six years old, simply walked away without a backward look. She couldn't even remember what her biological mother looked like, but she recalled everything about Patricia Boudreau. Glancing around, she half expected to see the Boudreau matriarch standing outside the car window, arms crossed over her bosom, her toes tapping against the asphalt in those low-heeled pumps she favored.

Liam blew out a deep sigh and adjusted on the seat, shifting to face her more fully. "How did it come to this, baby? I need to know what changed because something did. You wouldn't have known how to fake your death. Something like that takes time and know-how. And money, probably lots of money to bribe the right people, grease the squeaky wheels. Don't you at least owe me an explanation?"

Her breath caught in her throat when he called her baby. She knew he probably didn't mean anything by it. It was the one endearment he'd always called her. He'd teased her, saying he might forget her name when they were old and gray, but he'd never forget to call her baby because she was his. She'd called him honey and teased him that one day she'd have a *honey-do list* for him once they were married.

"It's a long story and not a pretty one."

"I've got all the time in the world, as long as you tell me the truth."

Liam's whispered words washed over her. *The truth*. The truth was ugly, as she'd learned when she'd been a naïve seventeen-year-old who'd never expected her whole world to be turned upside down. A girl who'd had to face the singular fact that everyone she loved would be in danger if she stayed in Shiloh Springs.

"Okay, Liam. I'll tell you everything I can. But first, can you tell me how my dad's doing?"

She forced herself to stay still beneath his steady scrutiny. Could he read how much seeing him again was tearing her up inside? She'd forced herself not to search the internet to find out about anyone in Shiloh Springs. Not that she hadn't

31

wanted to—the not knowing nearly killed her because he was so close and yet so far away. But the people hunting her had tentacles everywhere, and she couldn't risk pointing them in the direction of the people who meant the most, including her father.

"He was broken when you died. You were his whole world, and he simply went through the motions with you gone. About six months after your death, he decided he couldn't stay in Shiloh Springs. It was too painful. Too many memories. He packed up everything, sold the house, and moved to Oregon to be closer to his sister."

"I'm glad he had Aunt Lisa."

"He calls Momma once or twice a year, but as far as I know, he hasn't kept in touch with anybody else in Shiloh Springs."

Her chest burned, heart breaking for the pain she'd caused her father. Well, her stepfather actually, though she hadn't known that. Not until that awful day when she'd learned her family's truth, and her world had been blown to smithereens.

Ruby loved Sam Bright. He'd been her rock, the one person she'd depended on, counted on when her mother disappeared out of her life permanently. He'd held her when she cried. Sam made sure she went to school and helped her with her homework. And he'd loved her, never once admitting she wasn't his biological daughter.

"I never wanted to hurt Dad. That was one of the hardest things I've ever done, leaving him behind."

"What about leaving me behind? Did you once think about how your death would affect me? Or did you even care?"

She started to reach for his hand but caught herself. Touching him would be a mistake. She didn't have the right. Not anymore. Liam's voice froze her to her soul, the anger no longer beneath the surface but clear in every word, each one bit off, enunciated between clenched teeth.

"I cared, Liam. I loved—"

"Don't use that word. You didn't love me. If you had, you wouldn't have put me through the agony of losing you. Did you think I wouldn't mourn you?

Shaking her head, she squeezed her hands into fists. This conversation wasn't getting them anywhere. Liam demanded answers, ones she needed to give him. But it wasn't that easy. If she told him everything, it would put him in the crosshairs of a situation he didn't need dragging into.

"I'm sorry."

"Sorry isn't going to cut it, Ruby. You owe me answers. I'm not leaving until I get them."

She opened her mouth, ready to spill the whole truth, when her cell phone rang, and she jumped. The unexpected sound echoed through the car because her phone had automatically connected to the car's Bluetooth. Glancing toward the display, she read her partner's name on the screen.

"I have to take this."

Liam didn't answer. He crossed his muscular arms over his chest and stared through the car's windshield. She couldn't simply ignore the call. Lucy wouldn't be calling unless it was something urgent. Right now, Lucy ought to be stuffing oatmeal raisin cooks into their girls, not calling Ruby. Which only reinforced something had happened, and she needed Ruby's help.

"Hey, Lucy, what's wrong?"

"Ruby, you've gotta get back here ASAP. Some guy showed up, demanding to talk to Katie. When she saw him, she turned ghost white. She hasn't stopped crying. She ran and tried to lock herself in the hall closet. I'm afraid he will try and get inside and drag Katie out. I called nine-one-one, and they're on their way, but this dude's scary mad. I'm afraid he'll hurt her if he manages to get inside."

"Make sure the doors are locked. You have Hank, right?" Hank was the name they'd given to the baseball bat they'd bought for protection.

"First thing I grabbed. Well, the second. I grabbed the phone first. I got Katie out of the closet and locked her in the storeroom behind the kitchen. The other girls are upstairs in their rooms, with the doors locked."

"Good. I'm on my way. If he tries anything—" The sound of breaking glass reverberated over the phone, followed by Lucy's scream. Ruby gasped, her hands gripping the steering wheel until her knuckles turned white. "Lucy?

Lucy, what's happening?"

"Start driving," Liam's voice broke through her rising panic, and she threw the gear into reverse, slamming her foot onto the gas pedal. He braced a hand against the dashboard.

"Liam—"

Ignoring her, he spoke directly to her friend and partner through Bluetooth. "Lucy, I'm Liam. I'm a friend of Ruby's." Ruby couldn't help but notice the slight hesitation before the word friend. "Tell me exactly what's happening. Was that glass breaking?"

"Yeah," came back Lucy's shaky answer. "He threw a rock through the window."

"Okay. Can you hear anything else? Or see the man who's trying to get Katie?"

"I—he's standing out front on the sidewalk. At least he's outside the fence. The doors are locked. I made sure. But now, with the broken window, I'm afraid he's going to get inside."

"You can see him though?"

"Um, yeah."

"Does he have anything in his hands, any kind of weapon? A gun or a knife? A tire iron? Anything?"

There was a long pause, and Ruby's heart stuttered inside her chest like she'd run a marathon. It felt like it was about to jump out of her chest, beating fast enough she was afraid she'd have a heart attack. She heard footsteps on glass, the crunching noise eerily familiar, a memory she'd sooner forget trying to squirm its way to the surface.

"I don't see anything in his hands. He's pacing back and forth on the sidewalk. It looks like he's muttering something, but I can't make out the words."

"Alright. I want you to keep that baseball bat in your hands, and if he tries to climb through the window before the police get there, you swing it as hard as you can. Whatever body part comes through the window first, you pull that bat back and hit a home run. Can you do that, sweetheart?"

"Darn right, I can. Nobody's gonna get one of my kids. Does the imbecile think he will waltz in here and hurt one of ours? Not on my watch, he isn't."

Ruby let out a small chuckle. She was so proud of Lucy, of how she was handling this crisis. It wasn't the first time, and it probably wouldn't be the last, not in their line of work. But it was the first time one of them had been alone, without the other there for backup.

The wail of sirens came through loud and clear over the phone, and Ruby's hands loosened their death grip on the steering wheel. It was going to be okay. They'd get there and handle getting rid of whoever was after poor Katie. She was close. Only a few minutes, and she'd be home.

"Lucy, I hear sirens, so help should be there soon. Ruby and I are on the way, so just hang in there. You're doing a great job."

A soft sigh came through the speaker. "Ruby, cops are

pulling up out front. The dude's running. Oops, that had to hurt. A nice policeman tackled him, and he landed face-first on the sidewalk."

She looked toward Liam, forcing herself to maintain a semblance of calm. Never in a million years could she have dreamed up a scenario like the one happening right now in real time. Liam was seated beside her. Even though she knew she'd have to tell him at least a partial truth, the thought that he was here, sitting beside her, seemed like a miracle and nightmare.

She pulled the car up across the street from her house. From the outside, it didn't look like much. True, it wasn't in the best neighborhood in Wichita Falls, but that had been a deliberate choice when she'd rented the place. She hadn't been looking at anything fancy because that wasn't where the need was. The young girls who needed help didn't tend to come from high-end backgrounds. Mostly they were kids who'd run away from home, from situations that ranged from simple disagreements with their parents to unbelievable nightmarish and abusive conditions, the kind Ruby hated even thinking existed.

The two-story house looked a little worse for the wear. The bricks were cracked in places and yellowed with age. The roof had missing shingles in places, and a large blue tarp covered one of the skylights, which had broken during the last hailstorm. Hopefully, with the cash Gage had donated, she'd be able to get a handyman to look at replacing it.

While she loved the light it let through into the upstairs hall, maybe they'd be better off if she simply had it boarded over.

The windows had shutters, except for the one on the right first floor, outside the dining room. It had gone missing one night, and Ruby had no idea where it had disappeared to. The rest of them were dusty, and the paint was peeling. The brick-red they'd been painted years earlier had faded to a rusty color, which kind of blended with the color of the roof shingles. It wasn't pretty, but it was four walls and a roof overhead. Lots of people lived with a lot less.

Not waiting for Liam, she ran across the street and reached for the latch on the gate when she felt a hand atop hers. Even without looking, she knew it was Liam's.

"Hold up. You will have to talk to the police before they let you go inside."

"I've got to check on Lucy and the girls." She drew in a deep breath and straightened her shoulders, determined to get through this. It wasn't the first time they'd had problems here. Shoot, she had Officer Clancy's number on speed dial. Sometimes people thought a home run by women was an easy target.

They'd soon learned differently.

"Ruby?"

Looking up, she spotted Officer Clancy headed toward her. It looked like he was coming from inside the house. He'd have answers if anybody did.

"Can I go in? I need to check on Lucy and—"

"Everybody's fine. Lucy ID'd the guy who allegedly threw the rock and shattered the window." He pointed toward one of the squad cars parked at the curb, and she noted a young, dark-haired male seated in the backseat.

"Are you arresting him? He threatened the safety of everybody in my house. We can't let him get away with scaring them or returning and doing something worse."

"We can probably charge him with vandalism or maybe malicious mischief. Doubt the charges will stick, though. Lucy didn't actually see him toss the rock, so a lawyer could get him off without much trouble. The best I can do is keep him in a cell overnight. I wish I could do more."

She shook her head, knowing there wasn't anything more he could do. It was a shame the laws weren't stronger when it came to protecting the ones who needed it most.

"I understand. Do you need anything from me?"

"I think we've got all the info we need for now. I'll make sure you get a copy of the police report for your insurance."

She watched Officer Clancy glance past her, eyeballing Liam.

"You know our Ruby?" Though the question seemed innocent enough, Ruby knew it was Clancy's way of digging into her business. He'd checked up on her and Lucy, kind of like an honorary father figure, ever since the first nine-one-one call he'd responded to.

"Yes, I've known Ruby for a long time." Liam held out his hand to Office Clancy. "Liam Boudreau."

"Jonathan Clancy."

Liam nodded toward the house. "Things like this happen a lot?"

Clancy shrugged. "More than I'd like. Idiots figure women living alone are easy targets. We keep as close an eye on Ruby and Lucy as we can." He turned toward Ruby and patted her shoulder. "I'll have the station do a couple of extra drive-by routes for the next night or two, just to be safe."

"I appreciate that, Officer Clancy." When he shot her his patented glare, she corrected herself. "Jonathan."

"Let me know if there's anything else you need, Ruby. You've got my number."

"Thanks. I appreciate all your help. I need to check on Lucy and the girls."

"Of course. Give me a call in the morning."

"I will." She watched Officer Clancy walk away to talk with a uniform handling the nosy spectators. She wrapped her arms around herself like a shield to keep the world at bay.

He couldn't help feeling sorry for her. Her night hadn't been a cakewalk, between his shocking appearance and coming home to utter chaos. Maybe he should give her a break. But only for the night. Tomorrow, he'd show up on her doorstep and get the answers he deserved.

"Ruby, I see you've got your hands full. I'm going to go, so you can talk with your business partner and get everything handled that you need. Unless you want me to stay?"

Blinking up at him, he wondered if she even heard him. Her expression was vacant before she gave herself a little shake.

"Maybe you can come back tomorrow?" He heard the plea in her voice, though she didn't come right out and beg. Not that she would, unless she'd changed a lot. "You'll get your answers. I just...I need to deal with all this."

"Do whatever you need to do. I'll be here bright and early. Have a good night, Ruby."

"Good night, Liam." She turned and walked through the front door without another word, closing it gently behind her.

Raising his hand, he allowed his fingertips to touch the front door lightly. Ruby was here, alive. He could wait until tomorrow, but he'd be darned if he'd wait any longer.

He'd get his answers, no matter what it took. No exceptions. No evasions. No lies. It was time to take his life back.

CHAPTER FOUR

L IAM CLOSED THE door to the motel room, eyeing the side-by-side queen-sized beds. A wave of exhaustion struck, and he sank onto the foot of the closest one. He'd planned on driving back to Shiloh Springs after meeting with Brian, but that plan had been shot to pieces the minute he'd seen Ruby.

Running a hand through his hair, he sighed, wondering exactly how to process everything that had happened in the span of a few hours. His head still reeled with the fact Ruby was alive. Even after seeing the picture and having Brian confirm the facts, a part of him hadn't believed Ruby could be alive. The Ruby he remembered, the woman he'd loved, wouldn't have lied to him. She wouldn't have allowed him to believe she was dead.

He still didn't have an explanation for anything. When he'd slid into Ruby's car, he was sure she'd been about to tell him everything. Then her friend and apparent partner called, and the rest of the night had been utter chaos. Now he was no closer to the truth than he'd been—except he'd seen her and touched her. Heard the voice which had haunted his dreams almost every night.

"She's alive." He murmured the words aloud, allowing the reality to seep into his bones. Saying it made it feel real.

The trill of his cell phone startled him, and he recognized the ringtone. He'd set a specific one for his momma, and there was no hiding from her. When he'd left to meet Brian here in Wichita Falls, she'd made him promise he'd call. He understood. His mother had adored Ruby, and she'd been devastated when she'd "died." Now she wanted the truth, the same as Liam. At least he could assuage one of her doubts. Ruby was most definitely alive.

"Hi, Momma."

"Well? What did Brian say? Is it true? Is Ruby alive?"

His mother's rapid-fire questions made him smile. He could picture her sitting in the living room's big easy chair, a glass of ice water beside her and her laptop on the ottoman. Typically, in the evenings, after the hectic workday and once she fed whichever stray sons showed up at the Big House, she'd snuggle into the oversized chair and spend time going over things from the real estate company she ran and getting things ready for the next day.

"She's alive, Momma. I saw her. Talked to her." Hearing his mother's shocked intake of breath, he continued before she could begin another barrage of questions. "She's living here in Wichita Falls. I didn't get many answers yet, but we're going to talk in the morning. There was a bit of a dustup where she lives, something she had to deal with tonight, so I backed off. But I promise I'm going to get answers tomorrow."

His mother was silent for a moment, and he knew she tried to digest the fact Ruby not only was alive, but she'd lied to them for years. Would she ever have told them the truth, or would they have spent the rest of their lives thinking she was buried in the cemetery in Shiloh Springs?

"She's okay? You said something happened where she lives?"

"She helps run some kind of halfway house or something for teenagers and young adults who need help or are in trouble. Homeless kids who need a place to sleep for a couple nights or runaways they try to help get back home. According to the police officer I talked with, one of the girls' boyfriends tried to get in and make her leave. He tossed a brick or a rock or something through the window. Everybody was okay, and they will keep the guy in jail overnight, get him to cool down."

"Helping others in need. That sounds like something Ruby would be involved with." Her words cut off, and Liam heard another voice in the background. Sounded like his dad. Momma must've put her hand over the phone because their conversation was muffled, and he waited, knowing she wasn't done talking to him.

"Sorry, your dad wanted to know what you found out. Now, where were we?"

"Talking about Ruby's problem. I'm heading back over

there in the morning, and I'm going to get answers. I think she'd have told me everything tonight if we hadn't been interrupted by the call from her friend or partner or whoever is helping her run the place. Momma, she's hiding something. I can tell. But I'm going to get to the bottom of things, get the truth, and I'm not leaving until I do."

"Good. I know Ruby wouldn't, heck, couldn't have pulled something as elaborate as staging her death without help. There's way too much we don't know, but my gut says there's something bigger going on, and I want to know what. I need to know if she's in trouble. If she needs help, you let her know that we're here. No matter what."

"I will. Oh, by the way, guess who I saw tonight?"

"In Wichita Falls? I haven't got a clue."

Liam scrubbed a hand across his face, his head hanging forward. He was tired, and it was already after one a.m. He needed to get some sleep before meeting with Ruby in the morning. Needed to be awake and sharp because he wasn't about to let her get away with evasions or half-truths. He was going to find out everything, the good, the bad, and the ugly.

"Remember Gage Newsome?"

"What? You saw Gage?"

"I didn't recognize him at first. Brian's the one who pointed out who he was."

He heard his mother's soft sigh. He knew she often thought about the ones she called her Lost Boys. The kids who'd been part of the foster boys assigned to the Boudreaus, who for whatever reason ended up not making it at their ranch. Sometimes because it was only meant to be a temporary situation. Other times, custody reverted to the biological parent, or another family members stepped up to take them. Occasionally the boys simply couldn't adjust to life at the Big House and went back into the system. It wasn't because of a lack of affection and love on the part of his parents because they loved unconditionally, with all their hearts and souls, and never turned away someone in need.

"I've wondered about Gage for a long time." Yeah, Liam read that as his momma had been worried and praying for Gage from the day he'd left the Boudreau ranch. She had a soft heart, one as big as Texas, and felt every loss deeply.

"Well, he seems to have landed on his feet."

"Did you talk to him? Find out what he's been doing since…" Her voice trailed off.

"Didn't get the chance. I did see him pass an envelope to Ruby, though. It looked like it was full of cash."

"Oh, the plot thickens. We've got a real mystery on our hands, son." She chuckled, and the sound soothed something deep inside Liam. "I know you'll call me tomorrow, as soon as you have answers."

"Yes, ma'am," he replied because he knew her statement hadn't been a question. If he didn't call, he wouldn't be surprised to find her on his doorstep as soon as she could drive between Shiloh Springs and Wichita Falls.

"Right answer. Your dad says don't worry about work; he'll make sure everything's covered until you get back."

"Thanks. I shouldn't be gone more than another day or two."

"Son, you take all the time you need. You deserve answers, so don't come home until you're satisfied with the ones you get. Oh, I forgot to tell you, Ridge and Shiloh assigned Destiny to start digging, see if she can uncover anything about Ruby's 'supposed' death."

Liam squeezed the bridge of his nose between his finger and thumb. "Momma, I thought we agreed not to say anything to my brothers until I'd had a chance to see if Ruby was alive."

"These are your *brothers*, Liam. They have a right to know. Every one of them cared about Ruby, too. Besides, we don't keep secrets in this family."

"Alright, just tell them to have Destiny be careful. I don't want to spook Ruby any more than I already did by showing up. The last thing we need is for her to take off again."

"I will." She was silent for a few seconds before adding, "Let Ruby know she can come home. If she's in trouble, or there's danger, we will help her."

Liam's gut clenched at the thought of Ruby being in danger because every instinct screamed that's why she'd left in the first place. There wasn't any other explanation. They'd talked about what they wanted after graduation when they'd been young and foolish. Liam hadn't thought much beyond making Ruby his wife, though he'd thought they'd get married and then go to college and continue their education. After that, they'd have a couple of kids, and life would be perfect. She'd claimed she wanted the same thing, but now he had doubts. Had she wanted the same things, or had she jumped at the first chance to escape from the confines of small-town life and leave it all behind? Of course, faking her own death might have taken things one step too far.

"Love you, Momma. I'm going to turn in and get some shut-eye. I need to have all my faculties sharp when I talk to Ruby in the morning."

"I love you too, honey. Please be careful. There's more going on here than we know; I feel it. If anything feels hinky, you call right away. Remember, you're not alone; your whole family is supporting you. And if I don't hear from you, I've got no problem siccing your sister on you."

"No, no! Don't you dare. The last thing I need is Hurricane Nica blowing into Wichita Falls."

She chuckled. "Get some rest. I'll let you know if Destiny finds anything."

"Night, Momma."

Disconnecting the call, he laid the cell phone on the nightstand beside the bed and leaned back against the pillows. Exhaustion weighed on him, and he closed his eyes.

Tomorrow, he'd get the answers he needed. *Watch out, Ruby, because I'm not letting you go. No more running, no more hiding. Let's see if the truth really does set you free.*

CHAPTER FIVE

R UBY PLACED THE platter of scrambled eggs in the center of the table, next to the stack of buttered toast. Fresh melon, strawberries, and pineapple chunks filled the green bowl she'd picked up at a garage sale, attracted to the color because it reminded her of Liam's eyes. She shook her head, determined not to think about him. Not until she'd gotten everybody in the house fed and moving for their day.

Lucy and Katie had left about twenty minutes earlier, headed for the police station to finish giving their statements. She shook her head, knowing things could have been a lot worse if Katie's boyfriend, though she hated to call him that, had managed to get inside the house. It had taken persuasion and promises to get Katie to agree to stay with them, with promises of safety, and it had almost ended up being a total disaster.

"Miss Ruby, the bacon's burning."

Turning, she smiled at Julie, the fourteen-year-old who'd been staying with them for the past two weeks. The first couple of days had been touch and go. She'd worried Julie would run away in the beginning. They weren't a jail, and the teens and young adults who stayed with them, even for short amounts of time, were free to come and go whenever they wanted. As long as they followed the rules of the house, they were welcome.

"I'm coming, sweetie. Thanks for the heads up."

Julie shrugged. "I like bacon."

"Me too." Reaching into the oven, she pulled out the pan and used a fork to lay the slices onto paper towels to drain before transferring them to a plate. She handed it to Julie. "Would you mind putting that on the table? I need to get the juice."

She reminded herself she needed to get to the bank some time this morning and deposit the cash Gage gave her the previous night. Unfortunately, in the commotion of dealing with the police, she'd forgotten about the envelope in her purse.

She thanked God every day she'd reconnected with Gage Newsome. When she'd first run into him, she'd almost panicked because it was a given he'd remember her from Shiloh Springs, and she couldn't afford to have word get back to the Boudreaus, especially Liam, that she was still alive. When he'd promised to keep her secret, it felt like fate had brought her a familiar face, somebody she could talk with about Shiloh Springs without placing everyone there in the crosshairs.

Everything she'd done, everything she'd gone through, had been blown to smithereens because Liam was here.

"Miss Ruby, do you want me to put the juice on the table for you? You've been standing there a long time."

"Sorry. Silly me. Yes, please take the juice." Glancing around the kitchen, she did a quick mental check, ensuring she had everything out to feed the few people still there. With Lucy and Katie already gone, that left Julie, Phyllis, and Susan.

Within minutes, the three girls were seated at the table with her, eating the breakfast she'd prepared. Susan's expression was sullen, and she hadn't spoken a word since sitting down. Ruby wondered what had happened because she'd gotten more and more withdrawn for the last two days. She had a sneaking suspicion Susan wouldn't be around much longer. Although she'd tried, Susan had never opened up about why she'd been living on the streets, and Ruby had learned early on not to push too hard. The young women they tried to help sometimes never stuck around more than a night or two, and they'd learned to accept it. As much as she wanted to help all of them, sometimes the best they could do was give the girls a full belly and a bed for a night.

But every once in a while, she saw the miracles. The ones who turned their lives around, called home, or found jobs. Learned to leave their abusers. Those few made all the work worthwhile.

They were finishing up breakfast when Lucy and Katie walked into the dining room. Katie's arms were wrapped around her middle, her face pale and wan. Lucy's gaze met

Ruby's, and she shook her head. Ruby knew what that meant, especially after her conversation with Officer Clancy the previous night.

"Y'all hungry?" Ruby gestured toward the table.

"No, thanks." Lucy drew in a deep breath when Katie rushed past her, making a mad dash for the stairs. Susan and Phyllis stood and quietly started clearing the table.

Lucy walked over and laid her head on Ruby's shoulder. "She's gonna leave."

"They're letting him out, aren't they?"

"Yeah. Clancy said he could keep him maybe another couple of hours, but they had to let him go. Katie's terrified and refuses to stay because he knows she's here. I can't blame her. Clancy said he's got a record of domestic abuse priors, but nobody's been willing to testify. He doesn't have any choice but to let him walk."

"I hate this." Ruby slipped her arm around Lucy's waist, her eyes glued to the stairs. "Did she give you any clue where she'll go?"

"Nope."

"Gage gave us a donation last night. Luckily, I didn't go to the bank yet, so I've got some cash. I'll give her what I can. At least it'll give her a head start, get her a bus ticket or something. I know she won't go to the local shelter because he's tracked her down there before." Ruby drew in a deep, ragged breath. "I hate this. We finally get her to agree to stay here, tell her she'll be safe, and this happens."

"Sister, we do the best we can. I wish we could help everybody and make life easier for our girls. At least we've helped some, turned around a few lives. Focus on the wins."

"Easier said than done."

Ruby headed up the stairs where the bedrooms were located. Stopping by her room, she opened the small safe she kept locked in her closet and pulled out the envelope Gage had handed her the night before. Her eyes widened at the number of hundred-dollar bills inside. This was much more than he usually donated, enough to give Katie money and keep their home running for a couple of months if they practiced frugality.

After a few minutes of conversation with Katie, it was apparent there was no changing her mind. Not that she blamed the young girl. Life was terrifying enough when you were young and vulnerable. It was far too easy to fall susceptible to the predators roaming the streets, preying on those too naïve to know what to look for and avoid.

All too soon, Katie was on her way to the bus station. Lucy volunteered to drive her and make sure she got safely onto a bus headed for anyplace that wasn't Wichita Falls.

Ruby glanced at the wall clock in the kitchen, swallowing nervously. With the busy morning, she'd been able to avoid thinking about Liam, about the fact that he'd be showing up on her doorstep soon, expecting answers.

She owed him the truth. Even she was honest enough to know he deserved to know why she'd run away from everything and everyone she knew. But telling him meant drawing him into the fiasco that was her life and exposing him to the possible danger he didn't deserve.

Maybe it'll be okay. Nobody's bothered me in a long time. Maybe they gave up looking for me, and I can...

She broke off the absurd thought because she was a realist and knew better. They'd never stop, not until they got what they wanted.

And they wanted—her. Or what they thought she had.

The problem was she didn't have anything. Nothing of value. Nothing that belonged to her mother's family. Everything she owned had remained in Shiloh Springs when she'd died, and she doubted her father kept anything. He'd removed every trace of her mother when she'd decided not to come home. Chances were good he'd done the same with her stuff. She knew he'd moved to Oregon to be near his sister. That's what Liam had told her the night before. He wouldn't have hauled her things across the country.

Didn't matter. Liam was here, demanding answers. And she'd give them to him. He deserved to know the truth. All of it. She only hoped he didn't hate her for her choices. Heaven knew she hated herself.

CHAPTER SIX

LIAM PULLED HIS truck to a stop across the street from Ruby's house. A large blue plastic tarp covered the broken window. Maybe he should head to the hardware store and grab a couple of sheets of plywood. He could have that covered in no time and keep the place safe until new windows were ordered and installed.

Stop it. It's none of your business. Let Ruby handle it however she wants. Don't butt in. She's not your responsibility, not anymore.

Climbing from his truck, he glanced up and down the street, noting the houses surrounding Ruby's. There was an air of wear and neglect pervading the entire neighborhood, as though they'd simply given up. Chipped paint, loose shutters, and roofs that needed replacing gave the homes a sense of despair. It wasn't that the neighborhood looked particularly violent, except for Ruby's broken front window. No, it was more a feeling of apathy, like they'd simply stopped caring.

"What's she doing in a place like this?" Shaking his head, he opened the chain-link fence gate and headed up the cement walkway. He couldn't help noticing the seams between each section had been ruthlessly denuded of any weeds attempting to poke their heads through the cracks. The grass was green, though it looked a little brown around the edges. Probably could use a good soaking rain to saturate the roots. Texas heat was never kind to residential lawns.

He paused when he reached the front porch, noting that, like its neighbors, could use a good sanding and a couple coats of paint. Working construction, he knew he could make simple repairs to the porch and have it in much better shape. It wouldn't take much. Except it wasn't his place to even think about doing anything. Ruby had made it clear she didn't need or want him in her life. She'd walked away without a backward glance.

All he wanted now was answers. He deserved them. When Ruby had pretended to be dead, she'd left him gutted. Devastated with a soul-deep wound that had never healed.

He squared his shoulders, marched onto the porch, and knocked on the front door. A niggling doubt rose, making him wonder if Ruby would be here like she'd promised last night. Or would she take the coward's way out and run?

A somber-faced teen girl opened the door. Long dark hair hung loosely around her unsmiling face, big dark eyes studying him intently. She couldn't be more than fourteen, fifteen tops. Yet there was a subdued sadness in her eyes that shouldn't be near someone so young and innocent.

"Whatcha want, mister?"

"I'm here to see Ruby." He smiled at the girl, making himself relax so she didn't see him as any kind of threat. From what he'd gleaned last night, this house was a place for girls and women who needed safe and serene. Not the bubbling caldron of anger churning inside him.

"Why?" She crossed her arms over her chest, her feet spread apart like she was the guardian of the premises, and she wouldn't allow anyone unworthy pass its exalted threshold. In some strange way, she reminded him a little bit of his baby sister, Nica. Not in looks, but in her need to protect those she cared about.

"Ruby's an old friend. She's expecting me."

"Okay, hang on a sec." Without another word, she slammed the door in his face, and he could hear her yelling for Ruby. He chuckled because she really did remind him of his sister. Nica had done something similar when one of the social workers unexpectedly showed up at the Big House, leaving the woman standing on the front porch while she'd hunted down their parents.

The door was flung wide less than a minute later, and Ruby stood there. Even though he knew she was alive and well in his head, the sight of her still hit him in the gut like a punch.

"Liam."

"Can I come in?"

She took a step back and motioned him inside. The night before, he hadn't come into the house, instead electing to let her deal with the chaotic events with the police and her friend, though he'd stay outside, making sure Ruby didn't need him. She'd had enough on her plate with the chaos; she didn't need him demanding answers on top of everything.

This was his first chance to see the place where Ruby lived. While the outside might look worn and tired, the interior was the opposite. Brightly colored furniture filled the living space. The sofa was a vivid red color, faux leather, and looked new. Several overstuffed armchairs were spread around, each with a colorful pattern. Nothing was matchy-matchy, yet it all blended in a way it felt welcoming and lived in.

Dark-stained hardwood floors extended throughout the living room and ran into the kitchen, which he could see past the dining room. He liked the place, though it was hard to imagine Ruby living here. She belonged in Shiloh Springs.

"You okay?"

"Why wouldn't I be?" She seemed puzzled at his question, so he clarified.

"Last night, things seemed crazy. With the cops and everything."

"Oh." She gave him a halfhearted smile. "We got it all handled. They're held the guy overnight, though I wish it could be longer. He's a bully and a predator, but Katie loves him. It makes it hard to get her to see his true colors."

The front door flew open, and the same young girl who'd answered the door earlier sprinted inside, slamming it behind her. She pulled off her hoodie and let it fall on the floor by the front door.

"Julie, is that where your jacket belongs?"

"Sorry, Miss Ruby. I forgot." Grabbing the hoodie, she hung it on a hook beside the door. Spinning around, she stopped, spotting him standing beside Ruby. "He's still here?

"Julie, this is my…friend, Liam Boudreau. He stopped by to visit for a little while before heading home."

Liam caught the not-so-subtle hint. Did Ruby think she'd get rid of him that easily? He wasn't leaving without answers, no matter how long it took. He had the feeling she wouldn't be able to hold out for long.

"Hello, Julie. Nice to meet you."

"Hi, Mr. Boudreau. You know Miss Ruby?"

"Yes, I've known Ruby for a long time. We grew up together in Shiloh Springs."

"Where's that?" Julie's head tilted to the side as she watched him, reminding him of a little bird. She was cute, though far too skinny. Was she getting enough to eat?

"It's close to Austin. Ruby and I went to school together before she moved away."

Ruby shot him a grateful look. Guess she didn't want the kiddo to know that she was officially a dead woman walking.

"Cool." She turned to Ruby. "Can I get a snack?"

"A piece of fruit."

"Aw, come on. Fruit stinks." Julie scuffed her foot on the floor, her tennis shoes making a squeaking sound across the floor.

"Fruit." Ruby's voice brooked no further argument.

Julie shrugged and walked toward the kitchen. He watched her pull an orange from a bowl on the table. Good kid, at least she wasn't trying to sneak something different than what she'd agreed to.

"You ready to talk?"

"Not really," she answered with a wry smile. "But I said I would give you answers. You deserve them."

"Do you want to do this here? We could maybe go to a coffee shop or something if you don't want little ears picking up anything they shouldn't."

"It'll have to be here. My partner, Lucy, is out, and I don't like to leave the young ones without anybody being around." She gestured toward the kitchen. "There's a small porch in the back if you want to sit out there."

"That'll work."

Pounding sounded from the front door, a fist banging incessantly. A yelled, "I'll get it," followed by Julie racing toward the front door. He followed Ruby into the kitchen, and she stopped, looking around like she was a bit lost. Understandable. He'd been upside down ever since he'd seen her the night before. He was still wrapping his head around the fact the girl he'd loved for so long, the girl who'd died in an accident, stood before him, a grown woman with an entirely separate life. One that didn't include him.

"Would you like something to drink? I can make coffee.

Or I think we've got some lemonade."

"I'm good, thanks."

"Alright." He watched her body go rigid like she was preparing herself for a physical blow, something he'd never do, no matter the provocation. Then she deflated like a limp balloon.

"I'm procrastinating. Trying to figure out the best way to tell you everything that's been happening since…"

"Since you died?"

She winced at his crudeness. Too bad, if she didn't like the truth, she shouldn't have done the deed.

Opening her mouth, she stopped when Julie came running into the room. "Miss Ruby, it's for you." She held out a large manilla envelope, with 'Ruby' written across the front, one of the padded kinds.

"How did you get this?"

Julie shrugged. "Some guy brought it to the front door. Asked if somebody named Ruby lived her. When I said yes, he told me to give this to you."

"Thank you, Julie."

"No problem. What did ya get?"

"I don't know, let's see."

Ruby pulled open the envelope and reached inside. When she pulled her hand out, all the blood drained from her face. Staring at him, she opened her hand.

Laying in her palm was something he never expected to see.

A bullet.

CHAPTER SEVEN

L IAM PUSHED PAST Ruby, racing for the front door. Throwing it open, he jumped from the front porch and sprinted across the lawn, frantically scanning right then left, looking for whoever had delivered the envelope. There was nothing to indicate anybody had been close to Ruby's house other than two kids on bicycles.

"Sorry, mister. The guy said it was a delivery for Miss Ruby, so I took it. He didn't make me sign nothing. He just grinned at me and left. Didn't wait for a tip or nothing."

The girl—Julie?—stood with her hands on her hips, glaring at him like *he'd* done something wrong. He wasn't the one who'd sent a lone bullet to Ruby. The thing was an obvious threat. All color had bled from her face when she saw the envelope's contents. He had to wonder if something like this had happened before.

"It's okay, Julie. You didn't do anything wrong. I wish I could've caught up with him, though. Can you tell me what he looked like?"

She shrugged. "Taller than me, but not a lot. He wasn't old like you. Might've been one of the guys from the high school. Black hair, brown eyes. He had on a Scooby-Doo T-shirt. Guess he might be considered cute, but he wasn't my type." She scrunched up her nose, concentrating hard, he figured. This was a temporary home; there were probably lots of people coming and going. So, it wasn't surprising Julie hadn't paid a lot of attention to a delivery.

"Let's check on Miss Ruby, make sure she's okay."

She nodded and walked back into the house, and he followed close behind. Ruby stood where he'd left her, still clutching the envelope in one hand and the lone bullet in the other. He couldn't help noticing the slight tremor as she stared at the clear threat, intended to frighten and intimidate. If that was the intent, it worked.

"Ruby?"

"Huh, what?" She jerked, her concentration shifting from the bullet to him, and he watched a shudder rack her body. Watched her shoulders straighten, that backbone of steel, and her entire demeanor changed from scared victim to warrior princess from one blink to the next. "Sorry, it just surprised me."

"Miss Ruby, what can I do? Want me to call the police?" Julie pulled a cell phone out of her back pocket and waved it. "Bet they'd want to know somebody sent you that."

"No!" There was a level of panic in Ruby's voice Liam instantly caught. She didn't want the cops involved. What had she gotten herself into that she couldn't trust law enforcement?

"Julie, why don't you let me talk with Miss Ruby? I'll make sure somebody starts looking for whoever sent this bullet, okay?"

Julie's gaze darted between Ruby and him, and he could practically see the wheels turning in her head, wondering if she could trust him. Smart kid, not to accept everything at face value.

"I know you don't know me, but I'm not going to let anybody hurt Ruby. I know people who can help her. My brother is a sheriff, I have another brother who works for the FBI. Another brother works with the DEA. Then there's the private investigator and another one who runs a security company. We will find out who did this and make sure they don't get away with threatening Ruby. Okay?"

A slight smile tugged at the girl's lips before she chuckled. "All those brothers working for 'The Man'? Bet you never get away with nothing around them."

Liam grinned. "You have no idea. I figured with all those brothers working for justice and the American Way, I didn't need to throw my hat into that ring. I work construction." He shrugged. "I like building stuff."

"Alright. I'll be upstairs." She glanced at Ruby, who nodded and gave her a shaky smile. "If you need me, holler." Without another word, she bounded up the stairs and out of sight.

"Looks like you've got a pint-sized guardian angel."

Ruby drew in a shuddered breath before answering.

"Sorry I zoned out on you. I guess this shocked me more than it should have." She held up the bullet, and he plucked it out of her hand before she had a chance to pull it back.

He studied it intently, biting back a curse when he noted Ruby's name written on the side in black. Though he wasn't sure the size or caliber of the shell, it was large enough that it probably wasn't purchased at the local sports store.

Pulling out his cell phone, he snapped pictures of it from several angles before he plucked the envelope out of her hand. When she started to protest, he shot her a glance that stopped her instantly. He placed the bullet back in the envelope with quick movements and shoved it into his back pocket.

"I need that back."

"No."

"Yes."

Ignoring the glare Ruby shot him, he slid a fingertip across his cell phone and hit the speed dial to connect him to the person he needed to talk with. Rafe would at least be able to point him in the right direction to begin tracking down the not-so-subtle threat to Ruby.

Rafe answered on the first ring. "Hey, bro. You back in Shiloh Springs?"

"No. Things are a little more complicated than I thought."

"How so? I mean, I know about Ruby being alive. Momma let us all know yesterday. Why didn't *you* tell me?

You shouldn't be handling this alone, Liam. I'd have been right by your side in Wichita Falls; you know that."

Liam glanced at Ruby as she walked into the kitchen and stood at the sink, staring out into the backyard. He hated the dejected slump of her shoulders but knew it wouldn't last. The Ruby he remembered wouldn't let life knock her down without getting back up, ready to throw the next punch. She wasn't a quitter, never had been.

"I needed to make sure it was real before I said anything. What good would it have done to tell you Ruby might be alive, only to find out it was all a nasty hoax somebody was playing? Somebody's idea of a horrible joke?"

"I get it, but Momma said you had proof. Said Brian gave you a photograph of Ruby, a current one. What other proof did you need?"

"Photos can be faked. Photoshopped. I needed to see with my own eyes if it was true."

"Well, now you know. You've seen her, talked to her?"

"Yes. I'm standing in her living room right now. I need your help."

"You've got it."

"Okay, hang on a sec." With a couple of keystrokes, Liam texted the pictures of the bullet to Rafe. "I just texted you some pics. What can you tell me about the bullet?"

"Bullet?" There was a moment of silence before Rafe answered. "Well, isn't that special? Somebody's got a warped sense of humor. It looks like a large caliber, probably a big game hunting type. Deer or maybe elk. It doesn't appear to be anything exotic or foreign-made. Let me pass this along to Antonio; he knows more about weapons than I do. If he can't figure it out, he'll have Derrick Williamson take a look. Somebody sent this to Ruby?"

Liam watched Ruby while Rafe spoke. She'd filled the sink with soapy water and was attacking the dishes, scrubbing hard enough she might rub the pattern off. Plate after plate got the same treatment: wash, rinse, and put into the dish drainer. Her spine was rigidly straight, her shoulders back. Everything about her screamed she was one ticked off woman. He bet if he could see her eyes, they'd be filled with indignation with a dash of fury. His Ruby wasn't one to stand by and let anybody bully or intimidate her.

Not my Ruby. I can't think about her like that anymore.

"Bro?"

"Sorry, Rafe. Yes, somebody delivered it to her a few minutes ago. One of the girls here accepted the envelope. I didn't catch a glimpse of the guy, but she said it might've been some guy from the high school."

"Probably got offered money to deliver it by somebody who didn't want to be connected to an actual courier service. I definitely wouldn't want to send a single bullet through the U.S. mail, that's a big ole no-no. I've seen it before: your perp grabs a kid off the street, offers them fifty bucks, maybe a hundred, and all they gotta do is deliver a package. Easy money for the kid and plausible deniability for whoever hired them."

"I'm having trouble wrapping my head around some-body threatening Ruby. Because, yeah, a bullet is a threat. Last night, the front window of her house got smashed, and today, she's dealing with this."

"Any connection between the two?"

"Doubt it. Last night's incident wasn't directed at Ruby. She's helping run a home for teens and young women, getting homeless kids off the streets. Some guy came after one of the girls last night. He's still locked up until later today."

"I'd definitely consider today's incident a threat. Has Ruby told you why she left? What was so important she faked her own death?"

"Not yet. That's why I'm here now. We were supposed to talk, to find out the truth. Only…"

"Bro, I don't know whether what happened today with this bullet and what happened when she was seventeen are related, but don't you dare leave without finding out what's going on. She can tell you, or she can tell me and the FBI. I doubt Antonio will have a problem sticking his nose into things. You know how he gets about people he cares about."

Liam almost laughed at his brother's threat. He'd specifi-cally called Rafe first because he knew Antonio wouldn't be content to sit on the sidelines about something like this. He wouldn't have one iota of guilt in steamrollering right over Ruby's protests to gain the truth. Honestly, he was holding

Antonio as his next go-to if he couldn't get satisfactory answers from Ruby.

"I'll keep that in mind. I've got to go. Let me know anything y'all find out about that bullet. I'm going to hang onto the original, unless you think I should call the local cops and give it to them."

"Give me a few hours and let me see what I can find out. I'll call as soon as I know something."

"Thanks. Oh, one more thing."

"Yeah?" Rafe drawled out the question.

"Find out anything you can on Gage Newsome." Liam heard Rafe's indrawn breath. Couldn't blame him. He hadn't thought about Gage in a long time. It might be a coincidence that he was in Wichita Falls and knew Ruby, but somehow his gut didn't think so.

"Gage? What's he got to do with anything?"

"He's here. In Wichita Falls. I saw him last night."

"Seriously? I haven't seen or heard anything about him since he left the ranch. How's he doing?"

"No clue, but I saw him meeting with Ruby last night."

"What? Wow, what are the odds?" The sound of shuffling papers was audible over the line, and Liam could picture Rafe scrambling for a scrap of paper on his desk to write the info down. No matter how many notepads his fiancée bought him, Rafe constantly misplaced them. Either that or somebody swiped them off his crowded desktop.

"Ruby changed her name and hair color. Gage wasn't

around the Big House for long, so he might not have recognized or remembered her. But it looked like he passed her an envelope full of cash last night. Another thing I've gotta get answers for when I talk with Ruby. I need to get off this call and get some answers."

"Call me if there's anything else I can do. And I expect you to catch me up when you've got all the facts about Ruby faking her death. This is a story I've got to hear."

"Thanks, bro."

Disconnecting the call, Liam glanced toward the kitchen, startled when he noticed Ruby no longer standing at the sink. Dang it, he'd only taken his eyes off her for a second, and she'd disappeared. He strode into the kitchen and looked around, trying to determine which direction she'd gone. The staircase leading upstairs was empty. The only other exit from the kitchen was the back door. Without hesitating, he yanked it open, stopping short when he spotted Ruby.

She was sitting on the steps of the small deck, a can of Dr Pepper in her hand. Without a word, he walked over and eased onto the step beside her.

"Was it true? What you told Julie about your brothers?" Her words were soft, but he knew what she wanted to know.

"Absolutely. Let's see. Rafe is the county sheriff."

Ruby chuckled. "Why does that not surprise me? That's who you called just now?"

"Yes. Rafe's going to see what he can figure out about the

bullet. Find out everything he can about it from the photos I sent him. He should be able to tell if it's something commonly available or a little more exotic. Don't worry; he'll keep things quiet." The unspoken *for now* hung heavy in the air.

"Alright. Tell me about the others. I've often wondered about your brothers and how they turned out. They were good guys, and I knew they'd grow into good men."

"They did. Antonio works for the FBI. Ridge runs his own security company, private and corporate. Also cybercrimes. Heath's DEA. Shiloh's a PI. Then there's Chance. Believe it or now, he's an attorney, the district attorney for Shiloh Springs. Lucas is an investigative reporter, which probably isn't a big surprise. You remember how much he loved writing, even as a kid. He's won some pretty prestigious awards for his stuff. Brody's the fire chief. He also does arson investigations for Shiloh Springs and some of the surrounding counties. Not that we have all that many arsons in Shiloh Springs, but he's certified to handle anything that pops up. Dane runs the ranch. Everybody helps out when we can, but there's a good size daily crew that works the spread. Gotta admit he's darn good at what he does. Nica graduates this year with double masters' degrees."

"You left somebody off your list."

He sighed. "Joshua. He hasn't been around a lot recently. He's Special Forces, Green Beret. Joined the Army, followed in Dad's footsteps. It's been a while since he's been home. I think Momma's worried about him."

Liam stiffened at the sound of footsteps behind him, fighting the instinct to spring to his feet and move in to protect Ruby like a junkyard dog. He relaxed when he spotted Ruby's friend, Lucy.

"Sorry to interrupt. I just wanted to let Ruby know I got Katie all set. She's on a bus headed for Chicago."

"Chicago?" Ruby met Lucy's gaze, and Liam could almost feel the expectant stillness of her body as she asked the question. "Was that her choice?"

Lucy nodded. "It was. She chose it even before we found out the next bus there was leaving almost immediately. Why?"

"Because that's where she's originally from. She told me her mother lives in Chicago. It means she's going home."

"Really? Aw, man, that's awesome!" Lucy rushed forward and wrapped her arms around Ruby. "You did it, Ruby. One more success. One more girl off the streets, away from all the predators and sleazy losers preying on the innocent. Woohoo!"

Ruby's eyes filled with tears, and she returned Lucy's hug. "This is the best possible outcome. She's gone home, and now she has a chance to turn her life around."

"I bought the ticket in my name, so her jerk of an ex can't find her. I wish the cops could keep him in jail for a long time, but it is what it is. At least he got locked up long enough to scare her straight."

Ruby pulled back, and Liam saw her bunch her hands into fists at her side. Another tell, one she'd had even when they'd been together years earlier. Whenever she was about to do or say something difficult, she'd dig her nails into her palms to avoid exhibiting emotion. Funny how he remembered that.

"Lucy, can you keep an eye on the girls for a couple of hours? I need to talk to Liam, and it's probably going to take a while." She shot him a look before she added, "Liam's somebody I knew a long time ago, so we're going to catch up on old times."

Lucy mouthed the word, "Liam?" A waggling of her brows accompanied it.

"Liam Boudreau. I'm from Shiloh Springs, Texas. I'm going to take Ruby out for coffee. If you've got any concerns, call the sheriff's department in Shiloh Springs, and talk to Rafe Boudreau. My brother is the sheriff and can vouch for me."

"I don't think I'll need to do that, but thanks for the info. I'm a pretty good judge of people, and you look like you're one of the good ones. A real knight in shining armor type. Bet you're one of those guys who climb the tree to get down the stuck kitten, aren't you?"

Ruby snickered behind her hand, her eyes brimming with laughter. He wasn't sure how Lucy knew about one of his more embarrassing moments, back when he and Ruby had been dating. But he played along because the memory made her smile.

"I've been known to rescue a stuck kitty or two. Mostly I call my brother, Brody, and let him handle it. After all, he's the fire chief. It's in his job description."

"Why am I sensing there's more to the story here than I know? Oh, well, it doesn't matter. You two have fun. I'll hold down the fort. I'm going to go and call the landlord and verify what time they're bringing out the glass to fix the window." She gave him a little wave, adding, "Nice to meet you, Liam Boudreau."

"You'll have to forgive Lucy. She can be a bit of a handful sometimes."

He shrugged before holding open the back door. "She seems nice enough."

"She is. She's the real backbone of this place."

"It looks like you're doing a good job here. Reaching out, helping people."

"Thanks."

An awkward silence followed, and he wondered what excuse she'd try to come up with to avoid talking to him. Didn't matter. Unless the house was burning down around their ears, he was getting answers today.

"You ready?"

"For what?"

"I told Lucy I was taking you out for coffee. I thought you might feel more comfortable talking in a public place."

"Liam, I—"

"Don't. We are going to talk. Whether it's someplace where you'll be around other people, that's fine. If you want to stay here, we can do that. But we are going to talk. No more excuses, no avoidance. Tell me what I need to know, and I'll be out of your hair once and for all."

Ruby closed her eyes and drew in a long shaky breath. "I guess it's unavoidable at this point." Reaching for her purse, which was looped over the back of a dining room chair, she looked him square in the eye, her gaze steady and determined.

"Let's go."

CHAPTER EIGHT

R UBY CUPPED SHAKY hands around her hot chocolate, letting the warmth of the mug seep into her. Though it wasn't cold, she decided if she was going to have to do a whole revelation of her life, she deserved something hot and sweet. She'd deceived herself into thinking she'd never have to have this conversation. Never have to face the man she'd loved with her whole heart and soul. Never have to see the hurt and disappointment in his eyes when she revealed all her lies and deception.

"July twenty-fourth." His voice was low, emotionless as he recited the date. That date remained etched in her memory because it was the day she'd "died."

"I remember. Liam, I want you to know, if there had been any other way, any other choice, I'd never have made the choices I did. Would I do it again?" She drew in a deep breath before answering. "Yes, I would."

"Why, Ruby? You still haven't told me anything that makes sense. This whole setup is far too complicated for you to have done this by yourself. Who helped you?"

She leaned back in her chair. This was it. The big reveal

she'd never seen coming. But then again, she'd never expected to see Liam again. Time to bite the bullet and get it over with. She winced at the reminder of what she'd received just a short while ago. Bad analogy.

"I need to start at the beginning. Go back to a couple of weeks before...well before everything. Two people approached me, a man and a woman, who worked for the government. They wanted to talk to me about my mom."

"What does your mother have to do with this?"

"Everything. She's the reason for all of it."

"Your mom's been gone for a long time. Since you were six."

A pang of hurt and guilt crept over her. She hated lying, and this was a lie she'd begun so long ago she'd almost convinced herself it was true.

"My father said she went back to visit her family in Poland and decided to stay there. Never come back. We were good together, just my dad and me. He made sure I knew he loved me and would always be there for me. Don't get me wrong, I loved my mom. She'd always been there for me, and then she wasn't. That's hard on a child, especially a daughter, because mothers and daughters have a special bond."

"I remember you told me she moved back to Poland to help with a sick relative or something. That she decided to stay there and wasn't coming back."

"Because that's what my dad told me. He also told me

there were problems with paperwork. Then he told me she had met somebody else and wasn't returning. Each different story somehow tied back into the original one and, to a little girl missing her mother, reinforced that she wasn't good enough for her mom to stay."

"Ruby—"

"Don't. Don't say anything if you want me to tell you everything." She lifted her mug, taking a sip of the now lukewarm chocolate. She grimaced, wishing it was still hot because she felt cold inside. So cold. "I was eight when I got the first letter from my mother. She didn't send it to me directly. I think she was afraid my father would destroy it without letting me see it. Honestly, she was probably right. Dad was angry with her all the time. I don't think he ever forgave her for leaving us."

Ruby stopped talking when the waitress walked over with the coffee pot, refilled Liam's cup, and placed another hot chocolate in front of her with a wink.

"You look like you could us a fresh one. Let me get rid of that cold stuff."

"Thank you." Liam smiled at the middle-aged woman. She'd been quick to greet them when they arrived, took their orders, and set them up at the back table. Ruby faced the door and had a good view through the large window, watching people walking past the diner, going about their lives without a care. She envied them that ease because her situation was anything but easy right now.

Instead of a regular coffee shop, she'd chosen a diner not far from her house for their talk. This place had a comfortable atmosphere, one she liked and appreciated. She and Lucy had come here several times and usually brought friends here when they needed to grab a quick bite. It was an excellent place to bring the girls and women they shared their home with because it was unpretentious and homey. She'd discovered that going to a fancy restaurant often made the women feel uncomfortable. The younger girls didn't like the stuffy atmosphere of anything fancier than an all-you-can-eat buffet.

Once the waitress walked away, she dove back into the story, needing to get through it.

"You mentioned a letter." Liam's dark-eyed gaze studied her over the rim of his cup. There wasn't any judgment in that look, only simple curiosity.

"She mailed it to Sandra Summers. Sandra was her best friend in Shiloh Springs, and she asked Sandra not to tell my father about the letter and to get it to me without him knowing. Like I said earlier, my mom was afraid he'd destroy it without me having a chance to read it." She gave a wry chuckle. "She was probably right. After she left, he packed away anything related to my mom when it became clear that she wasn't coming back. There wasn't anything in our house that might be a reminder she'd ever lived there."

"I remember how hard it was on you when she left."

She remembered, too, because she'd cried on his shoulder, and he'd held her. He'd been seven years old, and he'd been her best friend. Her only friend because she didn't want anybody else. Only Liam. Her heart knew how special he was, even as a little girl who should have been playing with dolls and thinking all boys were yucky.

"She wrote she loved me and hated she couldn't come home. Told me she wished things were different, wished I could be with her, but it was too dangerous. I remember those words because why would being with her family be dangerous? Of course, to a six-year-old little girl's brain, danger meant being hit on the head with a frying pan, like in the cartoons. Anyway, she begged me not to tell my dad she'd written to me and that she'd try to write again if she could."

"That's a lot of responsibility to put on a child. Plus, she asked you to lie to your father. The person who loved you and took care of you." Liam's voice held an understanding and care she hadn't expected, which was stupid because she knew him—at least the man he used to be—before she left.

"I did what she asked. There was no return address, no way I could keep in touch, but I'd get a letter every six months. Telling me she loved me. She missed me. How she wished things could be different because she'd never have left me behind. I cherished those letters. They were the only lifeline I had with my mom. Because I was naïve or stupid, or maybe because I was too young to realize how she was manipulating me, I did what she wanted. I never told my dad about the letters. To this day, he doesn't know about them. Unless Sandra Summers told him, but I don't think she would. She cared about my mother too much."

"I doubt your father knows. He was devastated, heartbroken when you…"

"Died? You can say it. I know what I did. How much I hurt the people I loved. Do you think it was easy for me, walking away from everything and everyone I knew?"

"You still haven't explained why. What happened to make you fake your death?"

She shook her head, refusing to let the memories of that awful day surface. "The letters continued coming, one every six months until I was twelve. Then they stopped. No explanation, simply cut off without any indication of why. Sandra never heard from my mom again either. It was like she'd fallen off the face of the earth. At first, I was upset. I felt like she'd betrayed me all over again. Then I worried something happened to her. Finally, I started to hate her because she'd made me love her, and then she was gone. And I couldn't tell anybody."

"I remember you changed. Of course, it was over the summer, so I didn't see you every day, but you were angry all the time."

She nodded. "I was hurting, my emotions all over the place. I wanted so much to tell you, but I'd promised I wouldn't. Mom said terrible things would happen if I told anybody."

"That's a terrible weight to put on any child, especially your own."

"It was, but you were always there for me. If it hadn't been for you, I think I'd have gone crazy. I felt like I was being pulled in a hundred different directions. I couldn't talk to my dad because he almost acted as if she'd died. He took down all her pictures and got rid of anything that belonged to Mom. I think her leaving, he looked at it as a betrayal. One time I saw him glancing at a picture of her, one he had in his wallet. He kept running his fingertip over it, and he looked so sad. I never told him I saw him."

She picked up her chocolate and took a sip, letting the still warm liquid warm her insides. No matter how many times she thought about what happened, she still felt all the emotions churn inside, like a riptide threatening to pull her under. Though years had passed, sometimes the wound was deep and fresh and as new as the day her mother left.

"Ruby, this trip down memory lane is nice, but you still haven't told me why you decided to fake your death. You left a town full of people to grieve. Your father. My family." He hesitated a moment before adding softly, "Me."

"I did it to save your life."

LIAM FELT A chill chase down his spine at her words.

"What do you mean, you did it to save my life? You can't

simply toss that statement out there without explaining."

"Remember the two people I mentioned, the man and the woman?" He nodded. "They came to Shiloh Springs specifically to find me."

Her eyes slid past him, and he heard footsteps approaching. He watched her carefully place her mug of hot chocolate on the tabletop, and she smiled at whoever stood behind him. Some second sense told him not to turn around, to let the other person make the first move.

"Morning, Ruby. What an unexpected pleasure."

The deep voice immediately alerted Liam, and his spine straightened almost imperceptibly. Whoever the male was, he sounded like he was well-acquainted with Ruby. He needed to play it cool, not turn into a neanderthal and go all caveman on some unsuspecting stranger.

"Hi, Gage."

Gage. Why am I not surprised it's him? Why'd he show up right when Ruby's about to tell me everything? Dude's timing stinks.

Gage hooked his foot around the leg of a chair at the table beside theirs and pulled it over, sitting down like he had every right to interrupt their conversation. Liam noted Gage's eyes widen when he saw his face, recognition causing the man's lips to curve upward in a decided smirk.

Liam Boudreau? Well, now's here a coincidence I couldn't have anticipated. What are you doing with the lovely Ruby? I heard you hadn't seen each other in what, ten years?"

"Gage. I might ask you the same. You hang your hat in Wichita."

Gage gently laid said cowboy hat on the table and leaned his chair back on two legs, eyeing Liam like the cat who'd had all the fresh cream. Satisfaction gleamed in his eyes, though Liam couldn't figure out what made Gage feel like he had the upper hand.

"I'm a bit of a nomad." Gage smiled as the waitress placed a mug filled with coffee in front of him. "Never in one place for too long. Imagine my surprise when I saw a friendly face. It was a nice blast from the past."

"Gage and I ran into each other here at this diner, as a matter of fact." Ruby smiled at Gage, and Liam clenched his teeth. He knew he was being a jealous jerk, but he wanted all her smiles directed at him, not somebody who'd barely been a blip on his childhood radar.

"Quite a coincidence." Liam studied the man he'd known in another lifetime, one where he'd been one of the chosen ones. He'd never understood how Gage had been at the Big House one day and gone the next without any explanation. However, he did remember how Gage's leaving had devastated his momma. The woman might have a will of iron, but that did nothing to negate her soft heart. Tall, with dark hair, piercing dark eyes, and a strong jawline, Gage currently had a smirk on his lips. He sensed an underlying strength beneath the casual way he sat, muscles coiled as if he was prepared for anything. A predator lurked beneath the sarcasm and humor, and Liam wondered if his current prey was Ruby.

Not happening, buddy. Steer your attention in another direction because Ruby's out of your league.

"Gage has been a godsend in helping keep our home running." Ruby shot a glowing smile toward Gage, and he practically preened beneath her compliment. Which only made Liam more suspicious of the jerk. His gut told him something was going on beneath the surface. He'd bet his new pickup truck, the one on backorder that he was still waiting for delivery on, that Gage had an ulterior motive for befriending Ruby. All his instincts warned him he couldn't trust his former housemate.

"How so? What's Gage got to do with you and the girls?" Ruby had mentioned how she and her friend, Lucy, were running an unofficial place where girls could come and stay and feel safe not having to sleep on the streets. He admired what she was doing, especially since Maggie, his brother Ridge's fiancée, ran and supported several places for abused women and their families trying to escape desperate and abusive situations.

"Gage and his friends provide donations, which help provide much-needed funds to feed and clothe the girls and young women. That money also helps with the rent payments and the utilities. My salary alone isn't enough to cover everything. He's been like our fairy godfather." A cheeky grin accompanied her words, and Gage laughed, a deep belly laugh that made him seem more relaxed.

"Remind me to put you in touch with Maggie, Ridge's girlfriend. She can give you lots of advice on this subject. Chance has worked closely with her, establishing and opening shelters for abused women. She'll be a great resource for any questions you have." Leaning back in his chair, Liam crossed his arms over his chest and pasted on a smile. "Donations? Are you her only benefactor, or do you solicit donors? Because I'd be happy to spread the word."

Gage picked up one of the plastic-coated menus and studied it. Liam had the feeling it was all pretense, that the other man's attention was one hundred percent on their conversation. Maybe he didn't want to answer the question. And wasn't that interesting? Scary, too, if the money he donated was dirty.

Finally, Gage tossed the menu onto the tabletop and met Liam's stare. "I've got a few friends with deep pockets. They never mind contributing to good causes and the lovely Ruby's performing good work. I'm simply passing along the help, hoping I'll gain a bit of positive karma. But enough about me, I'm boring. Tell me, Liam, how'd you reconnect with our Ruby?"

Heat rose in Liam's chest at Gage's use of the word *our*. She didn't belong to Gage. He froze when he realized she didn't belong to him, either. Not that she was a possession, he'd never felt that way. They'd been a team, equal partners with their lives planned out, the whole world ahead of them. Then the world imploded, and he'd been stuck in limbo ever since.

"That's a long story, something between Ruby and me. I only ran into her yesterday, so we're here this morning, catching up on old times."

"Just like us." Gage's chuckle grated on Liam's nerves. "Seriously, Liam, how are your parents? I've thought about them often. Sometimes I wanted to get in touch and see how they were doing, but...well, too much time passed. Douglas and Ms. Patti are good people, and I hope they're doing well."

There was something in Gage's voice, a kind of wistfulness that made Liam think his question was more profound than simply asking about acquaintances. He'd never known the details of why Gage hadn't stuck it out at the Boudreau ranch, but maybe his short time there had affected him. Of course, he couldn't see anybody coming in contact with his parents, who weren't changed simply by meeting them.

"They're fine. I spoke with Momma last night. I bet she'd love to know you're living in Wichita Falls. She's got a soft spot for her 'Lost Boys'."

"Lost Boys?" Ruby glanced between Gage and Liam, and he could tell she'd noticed the tension between him and Gage. It was kind of hard to miss.

"That's what Momma calls the ones who came to stay at the Big House but ended up not sticking around. There weren't as many as you'd think, with the overcrowded foster care system. Most of the tough cases got referred to our ranch. A few either got hauled back into the system or returned to their parents." Liam turned his attention back to Gage. "You weren't around long, so I don't remember why you left. What's your story, Gage?"

"Don't really have one. Like you said, some of us got sucked back into the system, whether we wanted to be there or not."

Before he could question Gage further, his phone trilled. Glancing at the caller ID, he noticed Chance's name. Since his brother knew where Liam was and what he was doing, it had to be important.

"Chance, what's up?"

"Bro, you've got to come home. It's Dad. He's in the hospital."

"I'll leave now, be there as soon as possible." Without another word, he hung up. He'd call Chance back from the road and get all the details of what happened, but his big brother wouldn't have called him unless it was serious. His gut clenched at the thought. Not his dad. The man who'd taught him everything and raised him to work with his hands and build something worthwhile. Taught him right from wrong. Gave him a sense of pride and purpose. This couldn't be happening.

Ignoring Gage, he reached across the table and clasped Ruby's hand. "I'm sorry, hon, but I've got to go. That was

Chance. Dad's in the hospital."

"Oh, Liam. Of course, you've got to go. Be with your family. You need to be there." She squeezed his hand tight, and he bit back the instinct to ask her to come with him. And wasn't that a stupid thought? She hadn't been a part of his life for the past ten years, and with one phone call, he was thrown back into needing her by his side, the way she'd always been.

"How bad is it?" Gage leaned forward, picking up his cowboy hat from the tabletop. "I know somebody who has a private plane. It can probably get you there faster than driving."

"Thanks for the offer. I'll drive." Turning back to Ruby, he added. "This isn't over, sweetheart. It's only a reprieve. I'll be back, and we will finish what we started. That's a promise."

"I'll be here." Her words were a softly spoken vow, and he believed she meant them.

"Ruby, let me give you a ride home. That way Liam can get on the road faster. Liam, I am sorry about your dad. Please let Ms. Patti...never mind, don't tell her anything. Don't even mention you've seen me." Liam barely heard the muttered, "it's not worth it anyway," before he slid from his seat.

"Thank you, Gage. I'll meet you outside." Gage glanced between the two before giving a jerk of his head and walking away. Liam stood, his thoughts on getting back to the motel, grabbing his things, and hitting the road. So, he was shocked when Ruby walked around the table and pulled him close, her arms wrapping around him. She held him for a long time, and he felt a warmth start in the middle of his chest and spread outward, a sense of peace settling over him.

"Please be careful. Call me when you find out anything."

"I wish…" His voice trailed off.

"I know," she whispered. "Things aren't finished between us, but your dad takes priority. I don't plan on running again, Liam. Take care of your dad, and then we'll talk. I promise."

"Thank you. Be careful around Gage."

She rolled her eyes, and Liam almost smiled at the sight. "Gage isn't going to hurt me. He's a big old pussycat. I think Lucy has a bit of a crush on him."

"Just keep your eyes open around him. Something's up with him. It's too much of a coincidence. Intersecting paths usually make a pattern, and I'm not liking the one I'm seeing." He blew out a long breath, knowing he didn't have any choice. He had to leave.

"I'll call you once I get to the hospital." He'd gotten her cell number the night before, and despite all the evidence to the contrary—ten years' worth of lies—he believed her when she said she wouldn't run again.

He turned and walked out of the diner without another word, knowing one thing for certain.

He'd see Ruby again.

CHAPTER NINE

L IAM PULLED INTO a parking space at the hospital and shut off the engine. Every worst-case scenario played through his head like a full-color technicolor flick almost the entire drive back from Wichita Falls. He was surprised he hadn't ended up splattered on the side of the road because his thoughts weren't on mastering his driving skills. In just over three hours, he'd managed to traverse the distance between Wichita Falls and Shiloh Springs. It had been a miracle he hadn't been pulled over because he hadn't cared about speed limits, flying down the interstates sometimes topping a hundred miles an hour. Instead, his sole focus had been getting to the emergency room.

Sprinting through the electronic doors, the first person he spotted was his brother Chance, his somber visage indicative of the seriousness of the situation. Then he noted the others, each familiar face etched with varying degrees of worry and concern. Tina sat next to Chance, her hand clasped tightly in his. Liam caught her eye, and she shook her head at his unspoken question.

He walked to his momma without hesitating and squatted before her, taking her hands in his. Her usually smiling face was expressionless and pale, but he couldn't help noticing the tremble in the hands he held. Finally, she mustered a weak smile and leaned forward to brush a kiss against his cheek.

"I'm sorry we had to call you home, but I'm glad you're here." Her voice sounded raw, like she'd been crying, and something inside him felt like it had died a little bit. He'd never imagined being here, seeing his momma surrounded by her sons and their fiancées, seated in a hospital waiting room. His bigger-than-life dad couldn't be hooked up to countless machines behind one of those closed doors.

"Any word yet?"

Lucas, seated to his mother's right, answered. "The cardiologist came out a few minutes ago. They're waiting on test results, but he's stable."

Since all the chairs were filled, Liam lowered himself onto the floor, sitting cross-legged before his mother. "Tell me what happened. He seemed fine when I left."

She opened her mouth to speak, and Lucas gently touched her arm. "I'll tell him." Lucas met his gaze directly. "Harry went into the office to ask Dad a question. You talked with him before you left about changes to the blueprints for a job. He said he needed clarification and went to ask Dad. Harry found him on the trailer floor with papers scattered around his desk. Said it looked like he started falling and grabbed for the desktop. Harry called nine-one-

one, and then he called Rafe. Said he didn't want to call Momma and get her upset if it was nothing."

"Where was Sheila when this happened?" Sheila was his dad's long-time assistant. She was an older woman who'd worked with Boudreau Construction from the beginning and probably knew more about the running of the company than anybody else, including his dad. Sheila was an honorary second mother to Liam since they worked closely together every day, taking a chunk of the burden of the day-to-day job off his dad's shoulders.

"She'd gone to pick up their lunch. Dad wanted a steak and cheese sandwich from that place he loves, and Sheila called in the order. He must have collapsed right after she left to pick it up."

"And he was fine before she left?" Stupid question, Liam realized as soon as she said it. Sheila wouldn't have left his dad if she'd suspected anything was wrong.

"She said they were laughing and joking, and everything was normal. She stayed behind after the ambulance came to take care of things. I've got orders to call her the minute we know anything."

"Did he wake up and tell the doctors what happened?"

His mother shook her head softly. "He hasn't regained consciousness since he's been here."

The door behind him opened, and Liam stood along with the rest of the family. He wrapped an arm around his momma's shoulders to give her his support and because he needed the connection to her. Whatever the news was, he needed that contact with his touchstone to the family, and that was Momma.

Dr. Gabriel Shaw closed the space between them. "Sorry it's taken so long, but I wanted to get the test results back before talking with you. First off, the good news. Douglas did not have a heart attack."

With his arm around his mother's shoulders, he felt her release the breath she'd been holding. Relief flooded him at the news. His big bear of a dad having a heart attack had honestly been the first thought to race through his mind when he'd heard he'd collapsed. The man refused to slow down and wouldn't let age stop him from doing anything.

Dr. Shaw held up a hand to stop the questions everyone peppered him with. "We did an EKG. It did show a bit of arrhythmia, but that's to be expected. We've also performed an echocardiogram. The next thing is a cardiac angiogram to see if there's any damage."

"You said no heart attack was the good news. What's the bad?"

Before he could answer, a blonde woman rushed through the doors, barely waiting for them to swish open. She didn't walk, instead raced across the floor, and threw herself into her mother's waiting arms, tears running down her cheeks.

"Nica, baby, everything's okay."

"I didn't get your message until after class ended. I got here as fast as I could." She dragged in a shuddering breath and wiped at her cheeks. "How's Dad? Do we know anything yet?"

Momma nodded to Dr. Shaw. Nica's eyes widened at the sight of the doctor, and an expression Liam couldn't quite discern raced across her face. He'd have sworn it was guilt if he didn't know better.

"Uh, hi, Ga...Dr. Shaw. How's my dad?"

"Hi, Nica. I was just telling your mother that your dad did not have a heart attack. We need to run a few more tests to ensure there's no hidden damage. But his blood pressure is extremely high. We got it down with medication, and he's stable. We're going to keep him here, at least overnight. I'm concerned because he was out for a considerable length of time, so I'm ordering a CT scan to check for anything. We don't know if he hit his head when he passed out. But, again, he is stable."

"I want to see him." Momma kept her arm around Nica's waist, but her shoulders were squared, and Liam knew she wasn't about to take no for an answer.

"Of course, Mrs. Boudreau. But only you. We can't let him get too overstimulated. If you'll follow me."

When his mother closed the door behind her, everyone started talking simultaneously, a mixture of relief and worry in his brothers' voices. He stepped away and pulled out his phone, texting a message to Sheila, knowing she'd be walking through the hospital doors as soon as she'd gotten everything at the job site settled. Giving her a head's up would keep her from worrying, at least any more than she already was.

"Liam?" Nica stood at his side, leaning her head against his shoulder. He'd missed her, since she'd been swamped, trying to finish up her last classes before graduation. Carrying a double load had been hard, but she swore it was worth it, even if it kept her from being home as often as she liked.

"Hey, Sis. You doing okay?"

"I am now, knowing Dad's gonna be okay. How are you holding up? Momma said you were in Wichita Falls."

"Did she tell you why?" He knew his mother told his brothers, but she hadn't mentioned telling his baby sister. "Let's go over here." He led her over to a couple of the vacated seats and sat beside her. "There's something I need to tell you, but you have to promise not to tell anybody. It's important, Nica. I need you to give me your word."

"Of course." She stared into his eyes, and whatever she saw must've convinced her he was serious because she nodded. "Whatever it is, Liam, I promise I won't say anything."

"It's about Ruby." He ignored her gasp of surprise. "She's alive."

"What? But that's impossible...isn't it?"

"Well, as I've recently learned, nothing is impossible. I've seen her, kiddo. Talked to her. She's alive, but she's hiding something. I don't know what, but I plan to find out. That's why I was in Wichita Falls. Because that's where Ruby is."

"Liam, that's…wow. But, how. I mean, we had a funeral and everything. How is this possible?"

"I don't know yet, but I will find out. I know it has something to do with her mother. She was about to tell me everything, then I got the call about Dad and left immediately to come home." He reached forward and cupped her cheek softly. "I'll be going back there as soon as I know he's okay. I just hope she doesn't run before I get there."

Nica looked over his shoulder, past him, and her eyes widened in surprise.

"I don't think that's going to be a problem, bro." She nodded toward the door. A tingle raced down his spine, and he knew before turning what he'd see. Or rather who.

Ruby.

CHAPTER TEN

WALKING THROUGH THE emergency room doors and facing the Boudreau clan was the hardest thing she'd ever done. The whole drive from Wichita Falls had been fraught with self-doubt, wondering if she was making the biggest mistake of her life. She'd probably been an hour behind him the whole drive here because she'd raced home, threw a few things into a bag, asked Lucy to handle the girls, and took off.

All she'd been able to think about was the look on Liam's face when he'd gotten the phone call about his dad. Larger-than-life Douglas Boudreau. A man she admired like no other for the love and sacrifices he'd made, he and Ms. Patti. They opened their home and hearts to boys like Liam, desperately craving someone to love them, treat them with respect, and teach them.

It seemed impossible to think Douglas Boudreau could be felled by illness. In her mind, he was invincible. Always there, always would be. The reality was nobody lived forever. This was ironic, considering the entire Boudreau clan thought she was dead until a few days ago.

"Ruby?" She heard her name whispered by several of the brothers, but she couldn't pull her attention from Liam. He stood beside a lovely blonde woman, and a surge of jealousy shot through her. She realized it was an unreasonable response but knowing it didn't change the fact. It took several moments before she realized the woman at Liam's side wasn't his wife or girlfriend. It was his sister, Veronica, Nica to her friends. Wow, the ten years she'd been gone had changed the youngest Boudreau. Even with tear-streaked cheeks, she was gorgeous. She remembered Liam mentioning Nica was graduating soon with double masters' degrees.

Liam closed the distance between them, pulling her off to the side, away from prying ears, though she felt everyone's eyes on her. She recognized all of Liam's brothers, but they'd all changed too. They'd matured and grown into their gangly limbs and gotten past that awkward teenage phase. Each one had a woman at their side. They must be the girlfriends and fiancées Liam mentioned.

"What are you doing here?"

"When you said Douglas was in the hospital, I don't know, something inside me said I needed to be here." She couldn't tell him the real reason—that she needed to be here for him.

"You know if you stay, everyone in Shiloh Springs will know what you did. Whoever you're running from, they'll find you."

"I know."

"Are you sure? Be sure, because it's not too late for you to sneak out right now. I can get my family to keep their mouths shut. Ruby, if this is going to put you in danger—"

"My choice." She reached forward and clasped his big, strong hand between hers. There were rough calluses, proving he wasn't afraid of hard work. Not that she doubted that for an instant. Liam had never shied away from a task, whether on the ranch, manhandling steers, or hauling two by fours on his daddy's job sites.

"Not if it puts you in danger. I forbid it."

She stared at Liam, wondering if he'd lost his ever-loving mind. "Did you just say you forbid me to do something? Firstly, you aren't the boss of me. Never have been. Never will be. Secondly, it's my choice, and it's time for me to stop running, stop hiding. You wanted the whole story. You'll get it, but now isn't the time or the place. Right now, you don't need to be worrying about me. You need to be here for your mom and your brothers. And your dad will need you here, taking care of things until he's back on his feet, not in Wichita Falls, chasing a ghost."

He studied her before squeezing her hand gently. "If you're sure." He drew in a ragged breath before giving her that slightly crooked smile she had always adored. "Honestly, I'm glad you're here, Ruby. I'm scared. Won't admit it to any of the guys, but he's my dad. I can't lose him. I can't."

"And you won't. Has there been any news? Have you talked to the doctor?"

He nodded. "The tests have ruled out a heart attack."

"That's great news."

"His blood pressure is high, so they are keeping him to run a bunch of tests in the morning. Momma's in with him now. I guess they'll be moving him up to a room soon."

He glanced at something over her shoulder and grimaced, jerking his head to the right. It wasn't hard to know what was happening behind her back.

"They're all staring, aren't they?"

Liam chuckled and leaned forward, placing his forehead against hers for a second, then whispering in her ear. "Can you blame them? It's not every day somebody comes back from the dead, especially in Shiloh Springs."

She took a deep breath and turned toward the crowded waiting room and gave them a wave of her fingers. "Hi, guys."

When the whole passel of Boudreaus crowded around her, she wondered if she'd ever draw another breath again. Instead, she was hugged, squeezed, and welcomed back without questions or recriminations. She knew there'd be questions later, especially given what most of these guys did for a living, and she'd figure out a way to provide them with answers. But right now, feeling like she belonged, was a part of something again, brought tears to her eyes. It was the oddest feeling, yet even amidst the chaos, she felt welcomed home.

"Guys, let her catch her breath; you're smothering her."

Liam pulled her aside and ran his hands gently from her shoulders down her arms and back again. A sense of calm permeated her, like she was warming from the inside out. She'd expected recriminations, accusations, and downright hostility when she'd showed up. But she should have known better, she realized, because these men were Boudreaus, and they'd been taught manners by the strongest Southern momma she knew. The same woman who'd helped Ruby during her formative years, when she missed having her own mother around. A lot of who she was today was due to the nurturing and loving soul of Patricia Boudreau.

"I know the doctor said only one visitor at a time, but I think Momma's gonna want to see you without the whole Brady Bunch ogling our every move. Come on."

With a hand in the small of her back, Liam led Ruby to a closed door and gently knocked.

"Come in." Liam's grinned at the command because that hadn't been his momma's voice. Nope, that masculine growl had been all Douglas Boudreau.

Ruby's brows rose, and she smiled on hearing the male voice she recognized instantly. Things couldn't be too dire if Douglas was able to bark out orders in the same gruff way she remembered. Liam pushed the door open and stuck his head around it.

"Hey, guys, somebody would like to say hi."

He took a step back, held the door open, and ushered her through. She took a tentative step over the threshold, and her breath caught at the sight of the man lying in the hospital bed. His wife was seated in the hard plastic chair beside it, her hand holding the big man's. Blinking back tears, she gave them a watery smile.

"Hi."

Ms. Patti gasped, springing from the chair, and was across the room before Ruby could do more than blink. Warm arms wrapped around her, squeezing tight enough she couldn't catch a breath. But it was okay because this was Ms. Patti holding her. Now it was too late because the tears she'd managed to fight back when the door opened were now streaming down her face.

"Oh, honey. I can't believe you're here." Ms. Patti stepped back and cupped Ruby's cheeks in her hands, her thumbs brushing away the tears, though she had her own streaming down her cheeks. "I want to know everything, and I mean everything. But not now. Right now, let me look at you."

"Honey, turn the girl loose and let her breathe. Besides, I need a hug too." Despite the wires and tubes connected to him, Douglas held his arms wide, and Ruby crossed the small space separating them and leaned forward, allowing those strong arms to wrap around her. Memories flooded her. Her visits to the Big House, family dinners and cookouts on the back patio, and Douglas operating the grill. All those memories Ruby had buried, pushing them down deep so she wouldn't think about all the things she'd left behind when she'd faked her death.

"Son, get another chair. Momma, sit down." Douglas patted the side of the bed, and Ms. Patti perched beside him. Then he pointed toward the chair she'd vacated. "Ruby, sit there and tell me what's going on. Just the highlights, because this medicine they're pumping into me makes me sleepy, and I don't want to pass out in the middle of things."

Liam walked back in with the extra chair and offered it to his mother, who refused. She claimed she was quite comfy right where she was. Ruby smiled because it felt like she'd never missed a beat, never lost ten years, and was right back where she'd been when she was seventeen and a part of this amazing group of people. But she wasn't, not really, and never would be again. Nobody would be able to forgive her for what she'd done. It was all too little, too late.

"First, Mr. Boudreau, how are you feeling? Is there anything I can do or get you?"

"Always such a sweet girl. Thanks, but no, sweetheart. I want to know about you. Because I've got to say, you're looking pretty spry for a dead woman."

She winced because hearing it put that bluntly made it all the more real. "I'll tell you everything, but," she paused, gesturing around the room, "we might want to wait until you're more settled. It's a long and complicated story, and you need rest."

"Ruby…"

"I promise I'm not going to run away. I'll be around

when you wake up and tell you what I can. Explain all the gory details of my fake death, the whys, and wherefores." She grinned and patted his hand. "It'll give you something to look forward to. And you need to follow the doctor's orders. Get some rest and take your meds. You know the same drill you'd give one of your kids."

Douglas shook a finger at her. "You always were trouble. Just like this one." He winked at his wife.

The door to the room opened, and a dark-haired man in a white doctor's coat strode through, an electronic tablet in his hands. He glanced up, frowning on seeing so many people in the room. "What happened to only one person?"

"Extenuating circumstances, Dr. Shaw." Liam gestured toward Ruby. "She's a family friend who just got into town and learned about Dad being in the hospital. I knew Dad would want to see her since it's been several years since Ruby's been in Shiloh Springs."

"Welcome back to Shiloh Springs, Ruby." He walked over and looked at the monitor at Douglas' bedside, and Ruby watched him type a few things into the tablet. "Well, Douglas, all your lab values look good. Your cardiac rhythm is normal, though your blood pressure is still higher than I'd like, even with the medication. I've scheduled a CAT scan of your brain in the morning. The nurse will be by in a few minutes to get you moved to a room upstairs. Do you have any questions for me?"

"Yeah. Once I have this CAT scan thing in the morning,

I can go home, right?" Douglas tried to fold his muscular arms over his chest but stopped when the IV line in his arm pulled. Ruby bit back a grin when he mumbled something unintelligible beneath his breath. She had the feeling they weren't words she wanted to hear.

"No promises. First thing, we need to get that blood pressure under control. The test results will give us a better idea if the blood pressure is responsible for your blacking out."

"We could do all this as an outpatient. I don't need to stay in the hospital. No offense, Doc, but I hate hospitals."

Dr. Shaw grinned. "I haven't heard that like a thousand times. Sorry, Douglas, but you'll have to grin and bear it for the next day or two. I'm pretty sure I've got a dozen or so people out in the waiting room who'll be more than happy to make sure you aren't going anywhere."

"You can count on that, Doc." Liam managed to fold his arms over his chest, a look of intimidation crossing his face. "Dad will stay put until you give him the green light to leave. Even then, he will have to take things slow and easy." The glare he shot his father's way brooked no argument.

"Everybody, calm down." Ms. Patti stood and pulled Dr. Shaw in close for a hug before patting him on the cheek. The look of surprise on the good doctor's face was priceless, and Ruby fought to keep her laughter from spilling forth. Seeing Ms. Patti again made her realize how much she'd missed the other woman's wisdom and guidance. Shoot, she'd missed her warm hugs and her chocolate chip cookies.

"Uh, Momma, I think you're embarrassing Dr. Shaw." Liam's voice was laced with humor.

Ms. Patti slammed her hands onto her hips and turned to face her son. "You stay out of this. If I want to thank the good doctor, I'll do it my way."

"Yes, ma'am." Liam held up both hands in surrender. Glancing at Ruby, he winked.

"If you have any questions, have the nurse contact me. I'll be around for the next couple of hours and can be reached by phone or text."

Opening the door, he stepped back to let the nurse through and left. The nurse looked familiar, and it only took a couple of seconds for Ruby to remember her. Wilma Jacobs, Kimberly's mom. She'd gone to school with Kimberly.

She stopped cold when she spotted Ruby, her eyes growing round. "Ruby? It can't be, you're—"

"Dead? What was it Mark Twain said? 'The reports of my death are greatly exaggerated.'"

"I hadn't heard you were back in Shiloh Springs. But honestly, I'm trying to process that you're sitting here when we attended your funeral."

"It's a long story for another time," Ruby answered. "Right now, we need to make sure Mr. Boudreau is comfortable and on the mend."

"Absolutely." Wilma Jacobs was all business now. "Mr.

Boudreau, are you ready to go? We're taking you up to the third floor. Room three zero seven."

Ruby watched her switch over to professional mode with an ease she admired. She might have been surprised, shocked even, to see a dead woman walking, but she handled it like a champ. But, of course, as soon as Wilma got close to a phone, she'd bet the word would spread through Shiloh Springs like a speeding bullet through a bowl of Jell-O. Nothing she could do about it but ride out the storm. She'd decided to come back home with a clear conscience because she was tired of running. Tired of hiding. Tired of never being able to have a life without fear.

Within minutes, the nurse disconnected the monitoring lines, had the IV bag draped across Douglas' chest and called for an orderly to help transport him to his new room.

"I'm afraid he shouldn't have any more visitors tonight." At Ms. Patti's harrumph, she quickly amended her statement. "Except you, Mrs. Boudreau. You can stay with him. If you'd like, I can arrange to have a cot or recliner brought into the room if you'd like to stay the night."

"Thank you, Ms. Jacobs. I'd appreciate it."

She stood at Liam's side as they wheeled the gurney past the waiting area and heard all the well wishes from his brothers and the women. She could feel the unconditional love and respect they felt toward their dad. It made her miss her father.

Who still believes I'm dead.

"Do you have a place to stay, Ruby?" Liam's softly voiced question pulled her from her thoughts.

"I—no. I'll check with the Creekside Inn and see if they have a room. If not, I'll…"

"You'll stay at the Big House. No arguments. We can protect you there if needs be. Tomorrow morning, we'll talk and make plans. Figure out where things go from here."

Closing her eyes and praying for strength to get through the night, she took a deep, cleansing breath and said the only thing she could.

"Okay."

CHAPTER ELEVEN

C OMING AWAKE SLOWLY, Ruby savored the feeling of the soft mattress and silky sheets beneath her. Snuggling deeper, she pressed her nose against the pillow, inhaling the scent of clean linen and a hint of—lavender? She didn't use anything lavender scented when she did the laundry for the house.

Memory flooded back, and she sat up, looking around. She'd spent the night in a spare room at the Big House. She'd followed behind Liam from the hospital, so she'd have her car available. Nica and Dane arrived within minutes of them, and Nica had helped her get settled for the night. She'd taken one look at Ruby's face and told Liam and Dane questions could wait until morning. When they'd started to protest, she'd given them a stare that would have made Ms. Patti proud, and they'd back down. Then she'd bustled Ruby straight upstairs and settled in, but not before giving her a long hug and whispering how happy she was that Ruby was back and a promise to keep her brothers at bay until morning.

The bright sunshine pouring through the gauzy white

curtains proved that morning had arrived, and along with it the end of her reprieve. Tossing back the covers, she swung her legs over the edge of the bed and stood, stretching, and warming up her muscles. She took a quick shower, put on the jeans and top she'd packed, brushed her hair, and headed down the stairs.

The scent of coffee tickled her nose before she made it halfway down, followed by the delicious smell of bacon, and was that cinnamon? At the end of the stairs, she paused, listening to voices in the kitchen. Nica's was easy to hear, and she was giving her brother a fit. Which brother was it? She didn't recognize their voices; it had been too long since she'd heard them.

"Come on in, honey, coffee's hot."

Ruby started at the sound of Ms. Patti's voice. She'd half expected her to be at the hospital with Douglas. Wasn't he getting tests done this morning? As she walked into the kitchen, her gaze landed on the microwave clock, and stopped dead. No, it didn't say one-thirty. That meant she'd slept through the whole night and the entire morning.

"Good morning, Ms. Patti." She accepted the warm embrace, wrapping her arms around the older woman's diminutive frame. Though she wasn't tall herself, Ms. Patti barely reached Ruby's chin. It didn't change the fact Patricia Boudreau was a dynamo in a small package. Even as a teenager, she'd had a hard time keeping up with the Boudreau matriarch.

"Good morning, Ruby." The kitchen table was crowded, every seat taken, and she heard voices coming from the living room. She wouldn't be surprised if most of the family weren't in residence today. Lucas held a pretty blonde woman on his lap, with her arm looped around his shoulders. Was that Jill Monroe?

"Hi, Lucas. Good to see you."

She heard several other greetings, too many to identify each one. Finally, Ms. Patti made a shooing motion at Antonio, having him vacate his chair, and made Ruby sit. A cup of coffee immediately appeared before her, as if by magic, followed by a plate holding the biggest cinnamon roll she'd ever seen. It was honestly the size of her head. She blinked, then looked at Ms. Patti.

"Courtesy of Jill's bakery. She brought food for the whole family this morning. For which I'm grateful because I needed to be at the hospital first thing this morning."

"How's Douglas?"

"He was sleeping when I left. They did the CAT scan and some other tests, and they wore him out. I left him in good hands. Heath and Brody are at the hospital, and they won't let him do anything foolish, like try to leave."

Her lips turned upward at the thought. Stirring cream into her cup, she took a sip and moaned. Oh, she'd needed that. Caffeine was her vice, and she didn't feel completely human until she'd started on her second cup most days.

"Where's Liam?" The words were out of her mouth

before she could stop them, and she felt heat rise in her cheeks.

"He had to run into town to speak with the job site's foreman and talk to Sheila. Ensure the jobs are covered, and let the crew know to speak to Harry or Sheila, and they'll get hold of him if there are any emergencies. He shouldn't be gone more than a couple of hours.

Taking another sip of coffee, she deliberately and carefully placed the cup on the table and asked the question she dreaded.

"I suppose everybody in town knows I'm back." She framed it more as a statement. There was no way somebody at the hospital the previous night hadn't spread the word they'd seen Ruby Bright alive and kicking instead of six feet under.

"Couldn't keep it under wraps for long. Rafe's in town, and he's fielded a half dozen calls. Of course, he's not telling them anything. He doesn't have any details to tell them anyway. Liam's been pretty tightlipped, even before you waltzed through the doors last night," Lucas answered, no accusation in his voice.

Why wasn't anybody yelling at her? Screaming, demanding she explain how she was there, sitting at their table, instead of in the cemetery?

"You'll tell us when you're ready, sweetheart." Ms. Patti's hand squeezed her shoulder gently. *Oh, no, did I say that out loud?*

"I'm gonna wait to hear your story firsthand because I've got questions. Sorry, but it's the nature of the beast—investigative reporter. I can't help digging because once I see a puzzle, I have to keep going until I solve it. But Liam asked us to wait. So, we'll wait."

"Unless you're in danger and might bring it to our door. If that's the case, I want to know now. I'll do whatever I can to help you, but I must protect my family first and foremost."

And there was the Antonio she remembered. Didn't Liam say he worked for the FBI now? She stared at him, amazed at how much he'd changed. They all had. Somehow life had continued without her, and the boys she'd known were now men. Strong, alpha males with lives and loves. They'd found happiness and love, and she was thrilled for them.

Had Liam found someone, too? They hadn't talked about anything genuinely personal. Did he have a fiancée or girlfriend like his brothers? Or a wife?

"Ruby? Are you okay? You're a little pale. Take a deep breath. You're safe here. Nobody can get on the ranch without us knowing. There are alarms and cameras. Breathe. That's good. Now take another one."

She stared into the face of an angel. Deep chocolate brown eyes surrounded by dark lashes, filled with concern. Brown hair the shade of her favorite dark chocolate hung down to his shoulders. She recognized the face, though it had matured and changed over the years. If he looked this good, she wondered what his twin looked like.

"Ridge?"

"Yep. Nice to see you, too. You okay now, sugar?" His thumb brushed against her cheek, the movement soft, yet nothing felt intimate about it. Instead, she recognized it for what it was, a comforting gesture from one friend to another. The sweetness of that moment had her blinking back tears.

"I'm fine." She looked around, finally meeting Antonio's steely-eyed gaze. "I will never knowingly bring danger to your doorstep. If I thought my being here would endanger anybody, I'd leave this instant. Though I might have to leave anyway."

"Okay." A smile spread across his lips, the grin lightening his formerly stern countenance. "Liam would kick my butt back to town if he thought I was harassing you." He pretended to look around before leaning toward her. "Let's not tell him."

"I need to get back to the hospital," Ms. Patti announced. "Douglas will be waking up soon, and I don't want him to be alone."

"I'll go with you, Momma." Lucas motioned for Jill to get off his lap and started to stand, but Ms. Patti stopped him.

"No. Y'all need to get back to your lives. Your dad's out of danger, according to Dr. Shaw. Go back to work. I'll call if there's any change. No argument," she added when her sons began to protest. "Ladies, the same goes for you. Nica will stay with Ruby."

"I will?" Seconds later, she was standing behind Ruby's chair. "Yep, I will. No problem. Me and Ruby, we'll stick together like glue." Her mother simply smiled at Nica's capitulation.

"Excellent. I'll be heading back to the hospital in exactly thirty minutes. Everybody can meet back here for supper at seven. The ladies from the church will be bringing food to the house. Nica, be nice."

Nica's hand went to her chest, and innocently batted her lashes at her mother. "What? I'm nice."

Lucas snickered behind his hand. Antonio moved beside his sister and put her in a headlock, rubbing his knuckles against her head. Nica squealed the entire time while everyone else laughed.

"Brat. But I love ya anyway. Call me if you need anything. I'm working from home. If I'm out, Serena can get hold of me." Antonio faced Ruby, and for the first time since she'd seen him again, he smiled. "I am glad you are home, Ruby. If there's anything I can help you with, let me know. I've got a few favors owed me, and I don't mind using them."

The unexpected offer surprised her. He'd gone from the thinly veiled threat only minutes earlier to a direct extension of an olive branch. The surprising gesture filled her with a sense of peace she hadn't felt in a long time.

"Thank you, Antonio. I'll keep that in mind."

Each son kissed Ms. Patti's cheek, and they and their fiancées and girlfriends filed out of the house, leaving only Ms. Patti and Nica with Ruby in the kitchen.

"Whew." Ms. Patti lowered herself onto a chair. "I love my sons, but they are like a bunch of old worrywarts. It makes it hard to breathe."

Ruby laughed aloud, watching Nica roll her eyes at her mother's statement.

"Wonder where they learned that particular trait? Oh, wait, I know." She pointed toward her mother behind her back, so Ms. Patti didn't see.

"You're not too old for me to put over my knee, young lady."

Nica flung herself into the other empty chair and exhaled a heavy breath. The hair around her face fluttered with the breath, and Ruby noted the layers of colors blending into a golden halo. The blonde strands were mixed with warm caramel tones and hints of red hues. The Nica she remembered had grown up, matured into a beautiful woman with the same strong will and determination she'd displayed as a rambunctious preteen.

"Sweetheart, I wish we had time to talk more. I want to know everything you've done since you left. And before you say anything, Liam hasn't told me any details. Pretty much all I know is you live in Wichita Falls and that you know Gage Newsome."

"Gage? The same Gage who lived here when I was a kid? Whoa." Nica leaned forward, placing her elbow on the table, and resting her chin on her fist. "That's some coincidence. I don't think any of us have heard from him since he left. It's been so long I barely remember him."

Ruby watched Ms. Patti's face when she mentioned Gage's name and saw a myriad of emotions race across, but the one that surprised her was the look of guilt the older woman could not completely hide. There was a story there, something that made her friend sad.

"We ran into each other several months ago. He's been helping me with the home I kind of run."

"Home?"

"Yes, ma'am. My friend Lucy and I rent a five-bedroom house, and we try to help teenage girls and young women who've run into unfortunate circumstances. We give them a temporary roof over their heads and try to give them options. Gage shows up every few weeks and gives us donations to help keep things going. He's also done some odd jobs around the place. For example, fixing the fence, replacing a couple of windows, that kind of thing."

Ms. Patti was silent, seeming to digest Ruby's words. Nica looked between Ruby and her mother, though she didn't say anything. Something about what she'd said affected Ms. Patti. Was it telling her about the house she ran with Lucy? Or, more likely, she mused, it was hearing about Gage.

"I hope we can talk some more when I get home this evening, Ruby. Right now, I need to get back to the hospital. Otherwise, my husband's liable to sneak out without telling anybody."

Nica snickered and nodded. "He so would. Momma, go. I'll keep Ruby company. We won't get into too much trouble. Tell Daddy I'll be by to see his later."

"I will."

When Ms. Patti walked out of the kitchen, heading for the front door, Ruby looked across the table at Nica. The grown-up Nica was so different from the young girl she remembered. There'd been enough years between them, they hadn't even been in the same school. She probably wouldn't even know her, except for Liam. Dating Liam had opened up a whole new world for her.

The roar of Ms. Patti's engine sounded, fading as she drove away. Nica grinned and clapped her hands together, the loud sound reverberating throughout the kitchen.

"Alright, Ruby, want to see what mischief we can get into?"

Ruby blinked at Nica's question, the contagious carefree humor, and *joie de vivre*. How long had it been since she'd done something spontaneous? Spontaneity might have gotten her killed. What would it hurt to give in, just once? One day, without thinking about the monotony of her life. The temptation was overwhelming.

Throwing caution to the wind, she nodded.

"What have you got in mind?"

CHAPTER TWELVE

L IAM PULLED INTO a parking spot about half a block from the sheriff's station. It had taken a couple of hours to get through everything at the job site and deal with the fallout of Douglas' collapse. He was surprised by the outpouring of good wishes from the employees and contractors, along with offers of any overtime needed to keep things rolling while Douglas recuperated.

Sheila had been beside herself, guilty that she'd left him alone, even though there'd been no indication anything was wrong. He shook his head. The woman had been getting his dad a sandwich, which he'd asked for. How was she supposed to know he'd keel over the minute she walked out the door? Nobody could have anticipated that because his dad was healthy as a horse.

Work was covered for the next few days, so he could concentrate on dealing with getting his dad back on his feet and with Ruby. Seeing her standing in the emergency room last night hit him hard. Though he'd only seen her hours earlier, he never expected her to show up in Shiloh Springs. Yet, he knew that she was there for *him*.

The big questions still plagued him, and he'd get the answers. His entire family had already called or texted, wanting to know what Ruby told him, which was *nada*.

That bullet, though? He couldn't help remembering the look on her face when she'd seen her name written on it. All the color drained from her face, and he'd been terrified she'd black out. But his Ruby was stronger than the veiled threat.

The other thing bothering him? The two people who'd showed up right before Ruby disappeared from his life. His gut told him they were government. Which probably meant feds. Of course, this happened long before Antonio went to work with the FBI, but Liam wouldn't have a problem asking him to dig into things if Ruby confirmed his suspicions.

Pulling the door open, he stepped through. Sally Anne waved at him, speaking into the headset she wore. He pointed toward the back, and she nodded, motioning him toward the hall. It looked like Rafe was in his office. Liam hadn't called first. On his way from the job site, he'd decided to stop in and see if Rafe had found out anything about the bullet. It was a long shot, but he was grasping at straws without all the information.

He stopped at the open doorway to Rafe's office. Rafe stood with his back to the door, phone to his ear. Liam bit back a laugh as Rafe nodded at whatever the person on the other end said. He did this several times. Did he think the person on the other end could see him?

With a heavy sigh, he disconnected the call and turned. He didn't seem surprised to see Liam standing at his door.

"Might as well come in." Rafe walked around his desk and plopped into his chair. "What a lousy night."

"What's wrong?"

"Besides Dad being in the hospital? Let's see. A car accident over on Old Mill Road. Thankfully no fatalities, but three cars were involved. A group of teenagers heading back from the lake. They raided their parents' liquor cabinet and had a private party. I had some unhappy teens and even more unhappy parents. One broken arm, two with bruised ribs and lacerations. It could have been worse, but the whole mess took hours to clear."

Rafe shuffled papers on his desk and picked up a couple of sheets stapled in the corner. With a flick of his wrist, he tossed it across toward Liam.

"What's this?"

"Everything I could find out about your bullet. Which, unfortunately, isn't much."

Liam scanned the sheet, looking at side-by-side pictures, the one he'd sent to Rafe with Ruby's name, and another which looked identical. At least to his untrained eye.

"Bro, I know next to nothing about calibers and cartridges and shells. Give me the Reader's Digest version."

Rafe chuckled softly. "Alright. This is a .308 Winchester Ballistic Silvertip. They are used primarily for deer hunting. The bad news is that this is very common and available almost anywhere in the United States. It's popular for hunters who use tree stands because it's fast and accurate. But because it's such a common make, it will be nearly impossible to track it back to a specific purchaser."

Liam bit back a growl. It was pretty much what he expected, but the knowledge didn't make the disappointment any easier to swallow. As a threat, it worked because it had spooked Ruby, which was the intent of whoever sent it. His hands clenched into fists. If he ever found the person who was heartless enough to threaten an innocent woman...

"I consulted with a friend at Fish and Game. They concur with my findings. Said trying to find who bought this particular ammo without any other information would be like looking for a needle in a haystack. I wish I had better news, bro."

"You did the best you could with what little info I gave you. I had a feeling this would be a dead-end but needed to check it out anyway."

Rafe leaned back and crossed his hands on his stomach, his posture relaxed, but Liam wasn't fooled. His big brother was like a dog with a bone when a mystery was afoot. Sherlock Holmes had nothing on Rafe with his stubborn determination, and right now, he was like a bloodhound on a scent. He could see it in his brother's eyes. For as long as he could remember, Rafe's eyes revealed his intent. And his brother couldn't lie to save his life. He couldn't even bluff when they played poker because the eyes gave him away every time if you knew what to look for. And Liam knew.

"Ruby give you anything else to go on? By the way, she's stunning." Rafe shot Liam a cheeky grin to go along with his words.

"You're engaged. You shouldn't be looking at other women."

"Ha. I'm getting married, not buried. I can still appreciate a beautiful woman. Tessa is more than enough woman for me, and I've been too busy dealing with wedding stuff to even think about anything else." Rafe glanced at his fiancée's picture on the corner of his desk, his expression softening.

"The wedding date's almost here. Are you ready for the big day?"

"Absolutely! If it wouldn't break Momma's heart, I'd grab Tessa and elope. I can't wait to make her mine."

Liam laughed, knowing Rafe was right. Their mother might let them get away with a lot, but she wasn't about to be cheated out of a big, white wedding, especially since Brody and Beth's had a small, family-only event. Rafe and Tessa's big day would be a big celebration; no holds barred. The rest of his brothers were falling like dominoes, meeting their soul mates, and it looked like there'd be weddings scheduled for the next year or two, at the very least.

Liam tilted his chair back on two legs and glanced at the papers he held in his hand, remembering Rafe's question about Ruby. The thought that she was safe at the Boudreau ranch settled the restlessness inside him.

"With everything that's been going on, I haven't had a chance to talk with Ruby. She's promised to tell me everything, but every time we spend more than a couple of minutes in the same room, somebody or something throws a monkey wrench into the works. It's like we're on a carousel, and I keep trying to stop and get off, but it keeps spinning."

"Want me to talk with her? Maybe she'd be more comfortable talking with a cop."

Liam remembered Ruby's reaction when the cops were at her house the night he'd found her again. "Don't think that's a good idea, at least not yet. She mentioned two people showing up right before her quote-unquote death, one man and one woman. Now that we know it was a hoax, they had to have helped her. Ruby wouldn't have known anything about faking records. The doctors at the hospital wouldn't have gone along with something that big, not without a very good reason. I'm thinking a bit of governmental overreach."

"Hmm. Sounds about right. Which branch and why, those are the big questions."

"Feds, probably."

Rafe nodded. "By the way, I did a bit of digging into Gage. There's nothing that stands out in his background. Basic stuff. Birthdate, some records from when he was in foster care including the short time he lived with us. Pretty much nothing unusual after leaving the Big House until he aged out of the system. CPS records show he went to live with a biological uncle in Kentucky, who stepped forward when he found out Gage was in the system. He attended community college in his hometown in Kentucky before transferring to state university. Worked a part-time job to pay for everything scholarships didn't. After graduation, he held down a couple of low-level jobs. Currently, he's selling medical equipment to doctors' offices and hospitals. I found a record for a Gage Newsome in the military, but after the first year, everything became classified, buried in his records. I'll admit that set my Spidey senses tingling because it's not something that happens often. If you're worried about him, you should have Destiny do a deep dive. Off the record, that's what I'd do because there's more going on with our old buddy than meets the eye."

"I already have Ridge and Shiloh searching. Destiny's looking too." He stood and tapped the papers in his hand against his thigh. "Thanks for the info. I need to get home and talk to Ruby. If there's been one threat, changes are likely there've been more she hasn't mentioned."

"Probably. Call me if you need anything."

"I will. Thanks."

Liam strode out of the sheriff's office, pausing long enough to kiss Sally Anne on the cheek as he passed by her desk. He stopped on the sidewalk and raised his face to the sunshine, taking a deep, cleansing breath.

It was time to talk with Ruby and get the truth. End the nightmare of the last ten years and start over again. He only hoped this new beginning had Ruby in it.

NICA GRINNED AT Ruby and twisted the knob on the radio, making the music louder. The thrumming beat of the bass reverberated inside the car as the wind whipped around them. Nica had lowered the top on her convertible as they flew down the main drag between Shiloh Springs and Santa Lucia. Nica had pounced on the idea when she'd mentioned she wanted to pick up a couple of outfits. Before Ruby could catch her breath, she'd been practically frog-marched out of the Big House and straight into Nica's little red ride and over to downtown Santa Lucia.

Luckily, Nica's friend ran a boutique resale shop, and she'd been thrilled not only to see Nica, but she'd even taken them into the back of the shop and allowed Ruby to look through the items that hadn't been placed out front for sale yet.

In this case, the price was right, and she'd been able to pick up a couple pairs of dressier jeans and two tops, which would get her through the next few days. However, she doubted she'd been hanging around Shiloh Springs long enough to need more clothes.

"This is great." Nica grinned at Ruby. "I don't get to hang around a lot of women when I'm home. Oh, sure, I get to see my brothers' girlfriends, and they're all great. But, outside the family, it's been tougher. Not living at home, I'm away more than here."

"I'd think you'd have tons of friends, having lived here your whole life."

Nica tapped her fingers on the steering wheel in time to the music. She seemed so carefree, loving life, not worrying about looking over her shoulder every minute. So different from the life Ruby had lived for such a long time. Always afraid. Never trusting anybody. It had only been in the last several months that she'd even thought about having a life where she didn't keep a bag packed and ready in her closet in case she needed to take off in the middle of the night.

"I've got a couple of close friends, but the rest are people I knew in school. I've lost touch with most of them, except to say hello when I visit. Quick weekend trips or when something happens in the family." Nica shot her a cheeky grin. "Which seems to be almost every time one of my brothers meets their soul mate. I don't think there's been a single time where it's been smooth sailing during their courtships. Of course, that's a risk you take when you're dating a Boudreau."

"Surely not all of them? Lucas is with Jill. They've known each other forever." She couldn't imagine Jill bringing any drama into her relationship. She was a sweetheart, kind to everybody she knew."

Nica snorted a laugh. "Ask her about it sometime. Things got pretty hairy. She was held hostage in her apartment by a man obsessed with her. Of course, he was a major drug kingpin, which might be why Lucas freaked out."

"Surely that's the exception. I mean—"

"Tina's former mother-in-law hired someone to kidnap her. Tessa had a crazy stalker ex-boyfriend, and her brother-in-law tried to kill her over money. Beth's ex-husband escaped from prison and kidnapped their daughter. Shall I continue?"

"Wow. Guess I fit right in since I'm the one who faked her own death and stayed away for almost ten years."

"Want to talk about it?" Nica kept her gaze straight ahead on the road, though her hands tightened on the steering wheel. Ruby was surprised it had taken her this long to broach the subject because the Nica she remembered was obsessively curious.

"It's complicated. I've started telling Liam more than once, yet something or somebody has interrupted each time."

"Are you afraid of what he's going to say? I know I was only a kid when everything went down, but I remember Liam was...I guess the only word that fits is broken. Something inside him was never the same."

Ruby sat silently, thinking about what Nica said. "I didn't have a choice. If I'd stayed..." Her words trailed off, and she shook her head. "It all comes back to my mom."

"Your mom? I don't remember her."

"She left before you were born. There are times when I wonder if my memories of her are real or simply my imagination fantasizing how things were. Making happy memories where there weren't any."

"I'm sorry, Ruby. I can't imagine not having Momma around. She's been the biggest influence in my life. Always there. I've never felt alone a single day of my life between her and Dad and the whole Brady Bunch hanging around."

"Ms. Patti is the single most amazing person I've ever known. More of a mother to me than I'd ever known. I honestly missed her more than anybody else."

"Except Liam?"

Ruby hugged her arms across her chest, her heart clenching at the memory Nica's words evoked. "Except Liam."

"Can I ask where you went? It couldn't have been easy. You were so young. I can't even wrap my head around leaving everything and everyone behind. Please tell me you found somebody to help you deal with things, because after the trauma of the accident, losing your home must have been overwhelming."

Ruby drew in a deep breath, hesitating how much to tell Nica. She couldn't tell her everything because Liam deserved the whole truth first. Every Boudreau would eventually know why she'd taken the steps she had, the good, the bad, and the ugly. And some of the times had most definitely been ugly. But what could it hurt to confide in Nica?

"What the heck?" Nica straightened in her seat, staring into the rearview mirror. "Ruby, make sure your seatbelt is fastened tight."

"What's wrong?" Her hands immediately checked the

catch, cinching it tighter.

"Maybe nothing, but this SUV's been behind us for a while, and he's sped up." Her foot pressed on the accelerator, putting space between her convertible and the huge vehicle directly behind them. The stretch of road had narrowed from four lanes to two, one going in each direction, and only the occasional car had passed for the last few minutes.

"Son of a biscuit! Hang on, Ruby, I think—"

A jarring impact thrust Ruby forward, her body stopped by the seatbelt. She gasped at the feel of the belt keeping her from being tossed against the dashboard and windshield.

"What was that?"

"They hit us!" Nica's foot pressed down hard, and the convertible shot forward, putting space between them and the SUV. With the car's top down, Ruby could hear the engine behind accelerating, knew they were once again gaining on them.

Nica's hand left the steering wheel long enough to hit a button on her dash. Her Bluetooth activated instantly.

"Please state a command." The automated female voice sounded through the radio.

"Dial nine-one-one." Nica practically screamed her request.

"Dialing nine-one-one."

"Please, please, please answer," Nica whispered, urging the dispatcher to pick up.

"Shiloh Springs nine-one-one. What is your emergency?"

"Sally Anne, it's Nica Boudreau. I'm currently driving toward Shiloh Springs on Old Silver Court. A black SUV just rammed into us from behind. They're still following us, and I'm afraid they will try again."

"Nica! What car are you driving?"

"My red convertible."

Sally Anne's voice remained calm, which was good because Ruby could hear a hint of panic creeping into Nica's. "Can you tell me exactly where you're at? A landmark or cross street?"

"I'm on the two-lane stretch just past the old mechanic's shop."

"Okay, hang on, hon, I'm going to get somebody there right away. I'm going to put you on hold for a second, but stay on the line, alright?"

Ruby's hands gripped the sides of the seat, her fingers digging into the leather upholstery. Her heart beat so fast she could hear the sound thumping in her ears. This couldn't be happening. There was no question in her mind they were after her. Nobody wanted to hurt Nica; she was everybody's darling. On the other hand, while she knew they didn't want to kill her, there were people who wouldn't mind a few injuries as long as they got their hands on her.

"Nica, you there?" Rafe's voice came through the speakers loud and clear. Ruby's eyes closed, and she prayed they'd get to them before it was too late.

"We're here, Rafe. Black SUV's been following us pretty

much since we left Santa Lucia. When the roadway narrowed down to two lanes, they closed in. Hit us from behind, gave us a hard jolt. I put on some speed, but they've got more horsepower than my convertible. And there's nowhere to turn off."

"Who's with you, Sis?"

"Ruby. I took her to Kendra's place to pick up some clothes. I never thought—"

"Save recriminations for later. I've got Dusty and Jeb on the way, with lights and sirens. They were closer. I'm on my way. You're doing a good job, Sis. Do whatever you can to stay ahead of them. Swerve into the other lane or onto the shoulder if you have to."

"I'm doing my best..." She screamed as the SUV bumped them hard, and Nica wrestled with the steering wheel, swerving all over the road before straightening out.

"Nica! Talk to me! What's happening?"

"They hit us again. Hard enough I swerved all over the road. Good thing nobody was in the opposite lane."

Ruby whipped her head around, trying to get the license number. Rafe would need whatever information he could get to track these guys down, though she had a feeling in her gut the SUV was probably stolen. She'd managed to get the first few letters when she saw a dark-haired man lean out the passenger window. The look on his face, the eerily confident smile, terrified her. But not nearly as much as the gun in his hand.

"Rafe, they're closing on us, and one of them has got a gun!" Ruby yelled the information right as the sound of a shot split the air, and the car swerved sharply to the right. Her head slammed forward against the doorjamb, and then everything went black.

CHAPTER THIRTEEN

AFTER LEAVING RAFE'S office, Liam climbed behind the wheel of his truck. He couldn't wait to get back home and see Ruby. She'd been asleep when he'd left early that morning, and he hadn't wanted to disturb her. Momma's report that Dad was resting quietly had eased his mind, though he had a feeling they'd be butting heads before day's end. Being sidelined would be rough on the old guy to begin with. Liam wouldn't be surprised to see fireworks shooting out his father's ears, since he was forced to be flat on his back in the hospital.

He looked up when he spotted Rafe racing out of the front door, making a beeline for his cruiser. Spotting Liam's truck, he froze, then turned and sprinted in his direction. Liam rolled down the window as Rafe reached him.

Rafe slapped his hand against the truck's door. "Come with me. Now."

Without waiting for a response, he turned and ran toward his car. Liam jumped out and raced after his brother. Rafe had never invited him on a ride-along before. And it wasn't like he was asking now. Nope, he'd demanded.

Something about the way Rafe looked told him more than words. Whatever was wrong, it was serious.

He slid onto the passenger seat as Rafe started the engine, peeling away from the curb almost before Liam had the door closed. Immediately the siren blared, and red and blue lights flashed like strobes. Bracing one hand against the dashboard, he managed to get the seatbelt hooked as Rafe slammed his foot down on the accelerator.

"What the heck, bro?"

"Got a nine-one-one call as you were leaving. It was Nica."

A painful squeezing in his chest followed Rafe's words. Was Nica in trouble? Momma stated she'd have Nica stay home with Ruby when he left earlier that morning. If Nica was in trouble, did that mean Ruby was too?

"She's supposed to be at the Big House. Something bad must've happened for her to call nine-one-one instead of calling you directly."

"I need you to stay calm."

Liam stared at his brother like he'd lost his mind. "How am I supposed to stay calm after you make a statement like that? All that tells me is that it's something terrible."

"Nica and Ruby went to Santa Lucia. Nica was taking her to her friend's store. They were on their way back when she noticed somebody following them."

"Ruby never should have left the house. Not until we know why she's been on the run for so long. Coming back to

Shiloh Springs, I worried it might draw a big bull's-eye on her."

"Yeah, Nica said she noticed a black SUV following them. When the four-lane narrowed down to two, the SUV tapped them pretty hard on the back bumper."

"Son of a—" Liam slammed his fist against the side door, his heartbeat racing, his heart threatening to beat out of his chest. "Can't you go any faster?"

"I'd tell you to cool your jets, but I'd be wasting my breath. Dusty and Jeb are on their way. They were closer, so they'll get there faster than we will."

"What did Nica do after they got hit?"

"Said she swerved but got control and hit the gas. Nica managed to put some distance between them, but that SUV had more horsepower, and with a bigger engine, it didn't take long for them to catch up. It hit them a second time."

Rafe stopped talking, and the only sounds in the cruiser's cabin were the radio's static. Every second ticked by with excruciating slowness. His brother drove with a controlled finesse like he'd done it a million times before. How could he be so calm, knowing Nica and Ruby were in that car?

"Tell me she isn't driving the convertible." That red menace was Nica's pride and joy. She'd gotten it for her twenty-first birthday, a gift from their parents, and you'd have thought they'd given her the British Crown Jewels. She refused to take it to school, claiming it wouldn't get much use since everything was within walking distance. Plus, she didn't trust her dormmates to keep their grubby hands off her keys.

Rafe's silence had Liam cursing beneath his breath. If that car took a hard enough hit from an SUV, it could crumple like a crushed soda can. A terrible thought popped into his head. The darned vehicle was a convertible—what if they were riding with the top down?

"Can't you call Dusty? See how far away he is?"

"Dusty will report in the minute he spots them. Let him do his job. I'm worried too, Liam."

"Why do I feel there's more you're not telling me? You might as well spit it out because I'm going to find out anyway."

Rafe huffed out a long breath. "Before the call cut off, Nica screamed, and—I thought I heard Ruby yell something about a gun."

"Somebody shot at them?" He scrubbed a hand over his face. "This is a nightmare."

Every possible scenario raced through Liam's head, his imagination working overtime. Somebody tried to force Nica's car off the road. Why? He couldn't imagine anybody trying to snatch Nica. Nobody was that stupid. The only other reality, the only thing that made sense in this twisted nightmare—they wanted Ruby.

How'd they find her? She'd been in Shiloh Springs less than twenty-four hours. Living in Wichita Falls, she'd found a new life. Felt safe. Had it all been a mirage, with somebody biding their time until they plucked her off the streets once her guard was down?

Of course, everything changes with the introduction of a gun. Whoever it was, they weren't playing. They were dead serious about getting their hands on Ruby. He winced, realizing that might not have been the best word choice.

The radio crackled, and Rafe grabbed it instantly, listing to a whole bunch of codes and numbers. Liam recognized Dusty's voice. He shifted in his seat, facing Rafe, trying to read from his body language if things had gotten worse. Unfortunately, all those codes were like gobbledygook, and he couldn't make heads nor tails of them.

Rafe physically relaxed in his seat, though he didn't slow down. He focused straight ahead and spoke into the mic.

"Ten-four, Dusty. We're about four miles out. I will be there in a couple of minutes. Brody and EMS should be along soon too."

"Don't worry, boss. Your sister and her friend are fine. Scratches and they'll probably have some bruises, but all things considered, they're good. That was some mighty fine driving your sister pulled off, by the way."

"Any sign of the black SUV that hit them?"

"No, they're ghosts. But we've got a partial plate from our passenger. I've already called it in to Sally Anne to try and run the plate."

"Bet it's stolen," Liam muttered, not surprised when Rafe nodded.

"Thanks, Dusty. You and Jeb secure the scene. If the car needs towing, call Frank or Dante, and have them handle it."

"Already done. They're on their way."

"Great. And I can see your lights. We're here."

Liam had the seatbelt unbuckled before Rafe completely stopped. He flung the door open and hit the ground running, stopping when he spotted Ruby, seated on the front seat of Dusty's cruiser with the car door open. She looked none the worse for the wear, and he slowed his pace. Stopping in front of her, he squatted down, brushing his fingertips against her forehead, noting the egg-shaped lump. It had already started bruising, though there wasn't any blood.

"You okay?"

Nodding, she gave him a tentative smile. "Not the warmest welcome back to Shiloh Springs."

"Don't joke. You could have been killed."

"Nica was amazing. Liam, she kept her cool the whole time. Even spotted that we'd picked up a tail before I did. Guess I let my guard down a little too soon."

Liam gently cupped her face between his hands, forcing her chin up until she met his gaze. "You shouldn't have to have your guard up at all. I think it's past time we talk. Once a doctor has cleared you, that is."

"I don't need—" He must have looked downright scary because she cut off abruptly and nodded. "See the doctor. Check. Sure thing. I'll do that. No arguments from me."

He looked around, noticing Nica seated in the other cruiser. She was talking to Rafe, her hands flying with every word. Biting back a smile, he knew she was okay. The family had always teased her about talking with her hands. It had infuriated her when she'd been little, and she'd struggled not to do it. He'd sat down with her one day and told her she needed to do it if it felt natural because nobody should tell her what to do. Liam told her that the family teased her because they loved her, quirks and all. It had taken a few weeks to finally convince her it was okay, simply part of who she was, and she went back to her usual buoyant self.

"Nica looks pretty unscathed."

"Like I said, she was amazing." Ruby grinned at him. "You should have seen her. I swear, if she was driving in the Indy 500, I'd bet on her to win the whole thing."

"Comes from growing up with nothing but brothers. We might have been a bad influence on her." Uncaring about the discomfort, he sat on the ground in front of her. Reaching for her hand, he held it gently between his. He needed to touch her. Feel her. Know that she was really there, really okay.

He stood when he spotted the fire rescue truck pull up, accompanied by one of the ladder trucks from the fire station. In Texas, you rarely saw one without the other. There were many reasons for that. Brody had explained that if patients were unable to walk or move on their own, the added personnel were there to help the ambulance staff get them loaded onto the gurney and into the ambulance.

He spotted Brody climbing from the truck and watched him glance his way before heading for their sister. One of the EMS workers came over and smiled at Ruby.

"Looks like you've had a rough afternoon. My name's Cliff. I'd like to check you over, take some vitals, and do what I can to make you comfortable. Can you tell me your name?"

"Ruby."

"Good. Okay, Ruby. I'm going to take your blood pressure. The cuff will squeeze some, but it'll only be for two seconds. Alright, that looks good. Can you tell me if you're hurting anyway?"

"Not really. Jostled around some, but I had my seatbelt on."

"She's got a knot on her forehead. Probably bumped it against the side of the door." Liam pointed to her forehead, where the wind had blown wisps of hair across her forehead, and he gently brushed the hair away.

"Did you lose consciousness, Ruby? How about a headache?"

"No and no. I'm fine."

"Yes, you are, but I still need to do my job." Cliff smiled, giving Ruby an appreciative once over, and Liam wanted to punch him in the face. Which was nutso because he had no right to feel this way. There wasn't anything between him and Ruby and hadn't been for ten long, empty years.

Jealousy was an ugly emotion, and he forced it down, refusing to give in to his caveman impulses to punch the poor EMT and drag Ruby back to his place and lock her away. However, the temptation was awfully sweet.

"Looks like you're one lucky lady, Ruby. But I think you should still go to the emergency room and have the doc look at that lump. Maybe get a CAT scan as a precaution."

"That's not necessary, but I already promised Liam I'd see the doctor. I don't have a headache, and I feel fine."

"Good, it can't hurt to get a second opinion. Liam, good to see you. Tell your parents I said hi."

"I will. Thanks, Cliff." Turning back to Ruby, he asked, "Will you be okay for a couple minutes while I talk to Rafe? I will have him take us to the hospital, so you can get that bump checked."

"Liam I really don't need to go to the hospital. I'm fine. Besides, I don't need a record showing up at the hospital in my name. I can't afford to draw any more attention to Shiloh Springs. I should probably get in my car and drive as far from here as possible. Look what happened. I almost got your sister killed."

Liam got right up in her face, a combination of anger and terror spilling through his blood. Was she insane, thinking she could take off, and make the danger disappear? He was terrified that if she did run, whoever had tried to hurt her today would find her and finish the job. Not going to happen. Not today. Not ever.

"I've got news for you, Ruby. You are not going anywhere. Today should have convinced you that whoever was after you all those years ago hasn't given up. You are staying, and you're going to tell me everything."

"I am?"

"Count on it, sweetheart. Now you're back, I'm not letting you go again."

CHAPTER FOURTEEN

THE STERILE SMELL of the hospital hit Ruby first, followed by the noise. The swishing of the electronic doors had displayed the waiting room of the emergency room. Liam ushered her straight to the reception desk, and she barely refrained from rolling her eyes at his bossiness. Though a secret little part of her was thrilled that he seemed to care. She wouldn't have blamed him if he hated her.

He still might when he knows the truth, a little voice taunted inside her head. *You're a liar and a coward. He deserves somebody better. Somebody who won't put him in harm's way.*

"Ruby, sweetheart, come on. They've got a room for you. The doctor's on his way."

Without a word, she followed Liam and the clerk back to a room filled with a bunch of scary equipment. She hated hospitals. Hated doctors too. Not them personally, because she didn't know that many. But she couldn't help having a flashback to the last time she'd been in an emergency room. A sudden thought caused her to freeze.

This the same hospital, the same emergency room where

her life had been destroyed. She'd done what she had to, to keep Liam and everybody else safe, but she hated every minute of every day since. Because she'd left her heart behind when she'd been whisked out of the hospital. She had allowed her life to be turned upside.

"Ruby, it's gonna be okay. Are you hurting? Maybe we should get the doc in here ASAP." Liam snapped at the clerk, who skittered out of the room, likely to light a fire under the physician. She didn't blame the girl; Liam sounded down-right scary.

"I'm okay. Sorry, I had a flashback to the last time I was in this emergency room."

"I didn't think about that when I insisted you come. If it's any consolation, I'm not going anywhere. Nobody's going to whisk you away, not under my watch." A quick grin accompanied his words.

Dr. Shaw opened the door and stopped short when he saw Liam and Ruby. "Sorry. I didn't know it was you. What's going on?"

"Doc, you remember Ruby. She was in a car accident with Nica a little bit ago."

"Nica? Is she okay? Has a doctor checked her?"

Ruby wondered if Liam caught the way Dr. Shaw asked the question and had watched his body language the way she did. Interesting. Did the good doctor have a special interest in Nica? At least to her, his concern seemed to be more than a simple medical question. Glancing at Liam, she concluded he was oblivious. Typical man.

"She'll probably be showing up here any minute. EMS was on the scene, and they were examining her when we left. I wanted to get Ruby here so somebody could look at the lump on her forehead." He gently pushed aside the strands of hair, revealing the bump.

"Well, that's what I'm here for." Dr. Shaw held out his hand. "Ruby, I'm Dr. Gabriel Shaw. Can you tell me your last name?"

She bit back a laugh and cut her gaze over to Liam. "Which one?"

"I'm sorry?"

"Private joke, Doc." Liam shot her a pointed stare.

Ruby shifted on the edge of the bed, uncomfortable with all the attention. "It's Ruby Bright. I used to live in Shiloh Springs a long time ago. I'm only here visiting."

"Well, why don't we take a look and let's make sure you didn't do anything worse than bump your head? Tell me about the accident."

Ruby sat on the edge of the bed, kicking her feet back and forth, only stopping long enough for Dr. Shaw to fit a blood pressure cuff on her arm. Felt the squeeze as it automatically inflated and saw Dr. Shaw's nod at the reading.

"Nica and I were on our way back from Santa Lucia when somebody hit the back of her car."

She looked over at Liam, wondering how much she

should tell the doctor.

"It's okay, Ruby. I trust Dr. Shaw. Tell him what happened."

"Thanks for the vote of confidence, Liam. And call me Gabe. Half your family does already." A quick grin accompanied his words.

"We were hit twice from the rear. The second time was hard enough that we swerved all over the road. I'll probably bruise across my chest from the seatbelt."

"Did the car crash?"

"No hard impact if that's what you mean. When they shot out the back tire, we spun around a couple of times and ended up with the backend against a tree."

Gabe froze at her words. "Somebody shot at you." He rounded on Liam. "What has your sister been doing that somebody took a potshot at her? I swear Nica's a trouble magnet."

Ruby raised her hand and waved her fingers at him. "Um, Doc, they weren't after Nica."

The anger faded from his face as fast as it had appeared. "Somebody's after you, Ruby?

"Confidential information, Doc." Liam crossed his arms and stared at the man, though it didn't look like the good doctor would back down under Liam's display of machismo. "And what's with calling my sister a trouble magnet? You know something I don't?"

Ignoring Liam, Gabe turned back to Ruby. "Anything

you say is confidential. HIPPA regulations ensure that. Plus, I'm excellent at keeping secrets. Anything you tell me goes right into the brain vault and stays there unless I can help. And, of course, I'm always happy to help the Boudreaus."

Ruby couldn't help noticing the smile that accompanied Gabe's words lit his face, taking him from a nice-looking man to one who was breathtakingly handsome. She glanced at his ring finger—nope, no wedding band there.

"Suffice it to say, I have a very complicated past, and it's catching up with me. Physically, I'm fine. I got jostled around, hitting my head on the passenger door. And before you ask, no, I don't have a headache. No, I didn't blackout or lose consciousness. Nothing's broken. I wouldn't even be here if Liam hadn't insisted."

"Well, I'm glad he did. Haven't you ever heard the expression better safe than sorry?" He shined a penlight into her eyes, and she blinked. When he gently probed the bump on her forehead, she winced. It didn't hurt, but it was tender, and touching it didn't help.

"I'd like to get a CAT scan just to make sure there's no cerebral bleeding, but I'm fairly confident everything's fine. Once you get the scan and we look at it, you can go home."

"Thank you."

"Liam, your dad's doing well. The test results we've gotten back all look good. I want to keep him here for at least one more night, but we'll probably send him home in the morning."

"That's great. Appreciate you're taking care of him, Gabe."

"It's what I do. I'll have somebody take Ruby over for the scan. Shouldn't be long." He glanced her way. "I promise, it's quick and painless."

As he left the room, Liam sat beside her on the bed, and she laid her head on his shoulder. All in all, it had been quite a day, and it wasn't even half over. She couldn't forget the look on the man's face, the one who'd leaned out the window before taking a shot at her. He'd grinned like he was having fun, like terrorizing two women was the best thing he'd done all day.

And he'd deliberately missed. Deep in her gut, she knew he'd pulled the shot, aimed low to hit the car's tire. The roof on the convertible had been down, it would have been so easy to aim at her, blow her head off. So why hadn't he taken the shot?

"Everything's going to be okay, sweetheart. We'll talk and figure out what's happening and what we need to do to make it all go away." She felt his fingers at the back of her neck, gently making tiny movements against her skin. It felt oddly soothing.

When the orderly came to take her for the scan, Liam wanted to go with her, but she assured him she'd be fine. He reluctantly agreed to wait in the emergency room and make some calls. She knew he wanted to check in with Brody and assure himself that Nica was alright. It seemed strange that they hadn't made it to the hospital yet and prayed nothing worse had happened.

The testing took over an hour before Ruby was wheeled back into her room. It was empty. Guess Liam didn't know she had been brought back to her room. Climbing back onto the bed, she laid back, pulled the thin blanket up to cover her, and closed her eyes. She was ready to get out of here but oddly reluctant because that would mean the Boudreaus would want answers.

She'd managed not to tell them anything, and circumstances had kept them from putting additional pressure on her. But it didn't take a genius to know today was the end of her reprieve. Today she'd have to confess to her actions, the good, the bad, and the ugly. Either that or run away, and she was tired of running. She'd been running for a good chunk of her life, and that was over.

The sound of the door quietly opening had her stiffening, though she kept her eyes closed. If it was Liam, he'd talk to her. Maybe call her name. If it wasn't, she wasn't sure what she'd do, but she wasn't about to lay there like a victim.

"Ruby?"

Her eyes flew open at the familiar voice, even though he barely spoke above a whisper. "Gage? What are you doing here?"

"The bigger question is, what are you doing here?" He stood with his arms crossed over his chest, a scowl on his face. If he was trying to intimate her, well, it was working.

"You know Douglas Boudreau was admitted to the hospital. I came to be here for Liam."

He shook his head and made a tsking sound. "Not what I meant. What are you doing *here*?" He emphasized the last word. "How'd you end up in the emergency room?"

"Would you believe a car accident?" She didn't understand why Gage was in Shiloh Springs. Until Liam showed up in Wichita Falls, they'd barely mentioned her hometown. So why was he standing here, in a place he'd sworn he'd never come back to?

"Are you hurt?" His eyes scanned her from head to toe, though he couldn't see much, and she pulled the blanket up to her neck. Had he never heard about invasion of privacy? They were friends. Nothing more. He helped with the girls, gave her donation to keep their project afloat, and other than the first time they'd met, had never expressed an interest in taking things further.

"The bigger question is, why are you here? You told me you'd never come back to Shiloh Springs. I think you said there were too many memories here, things you were better off forgetting."

Gage pulled over the rolling stool and sat beside her bed. "I was worried about you. After seeing Liam in Wichita Falls, you seemed different. I know I gave him a hard time, but that's personal. We've got history."

"You never mentioned you lived with the Boudreaus when we talked about Shiloh Springs. I always wondered why."

He pointed his finger at her. "You didn't mention being Liam's ex, either." Shaking his head, he chuckled. "Guess we're both guilty about keeping secrets."

They both turned when the clerk walked in, and she stopped, staring at Gage. Not that Ruby blamed her. Gage exuded an inherent sex appeal that would make him the proverbial chick magnet, though he'd never mentioned having a girlfriend.

"I'm sorry. I just wanted to let Ms. Bright know the doctor will be in shortly to go over her test results."

"Thanks. I'm ready to get out of here. No offense."

She smiled. "None taken. That's pretty much how most people feel about hospitals."

After she left, Gage picked up Ruby's hand, toying with her fingers. She felt like he was stalling, though she wasn't sure why. Every time they'd met, he'd always been up front and clear about the corporate donations, always teasing and making her feel special. Why was he acting like she was a stranger now?

"I talked with Lucy this morning. I heard about your trouble—the rock through the window. I stopped by and asked if you needed me to get some glass or maybe board it until somebody could repair it. Imagine my surprise when I found out you'd hightailed it back to your old stomping grounds."

"I had to. Seeing Liam's face when he heard about his

dad, I couldn't let him deal with that alone."

"Honey, Boudreaus are never alone. He's got brothers and a sister to lean on. He's got Ms. Patti. Haven't you heard the Boudreaus circle the wagons whenever adversity raises its ugly head and beats it into submission? Nobody, and I mean nobody, gets the best of a Boudreau."

She tilted her head, wondering about the bitterness in his tone. It didn't make sense. Knowing the Boudreaus, loving them, she couldn't understand the animosity he felt toward Liam. Or did it extend to all of them?

"Gage…"

"I'm sorry. It's been a long couple of days. I simply needed to make sure you were okay. Don't ask me why, but I had a bad feeling when I talked to Lucy. You never did answer me. Why are you here?"

"I did answer. It was a car accident. I got a bump on the noggin, and Liam insisted I get checked by the doctor. Nothing to worry about."

"Now who's keeping secrets? I saw the red convertible by the side of the road, where the wrecker was hooking it up to tow it in. Who was driving?"

"Nica."

"She's okay?"

"Far as I know, she's fine. The EMTs were supposed to bring her in. When I left, Rafe refused to let her bum a ride home with one of the deputies. She's probably around here somewhere."

Gage stood abruptly, his eyes scanning the room like he expected somebody to jump out at him any moment. She'd never seen the man seem so spooked.

"Listen, I know there's far more than what you're telling me, but it'll have to wait until we can talk later. Maybe when you're back home. I need to get out of here. I don't need the Boudreaus to see me, and I definitely shouldn't see them. I just want you to remember I'm your friend, Ruby. When all the dust settles and you come to your senses, you've got my number."

"Why don't you want to see them? I'm sure they'd be happy to find out you turned well. I bet they'd love to talk to you."

"Not a good idea. Too much water under the bridge. Just promise me, if you need me, if anything happens, you'll call."

She nodded. "I promise."

He brushed a kiss against her forehead, careful not to touch the bump. "Bye, Ruby."

"Goodbye, Gage."

He turned to leave but froze at the sight of the woman standing in the open doorway. Quickly spinning around, he pretended to be working on the monitor beside her bed. Ruby snorted, wondering why he thought that would work. He wasn't fooling anybody, and it finally dawned on him that his ruse wasn't working.

Drawing in a deep breath, he turned and faced the petite

woman, and Ruby wondered if he felt like a condemned man about to face a firing squad. Poor thing, he hadn't even gotten a last meal.

It was far too late for him to run, and Ruby hoped he was ready to face his biggest fear—because Ms. Patti was here, and she had a feeling nothing was going to be the same again.

CHAPTER FIFTEEN

RUBY WATCHED GAGE stand in front of Ms. Patti, the look on his face bordered on yearning tinged with regret. He'd been blunt when he showed up at the emergency room. Emphatic in his demand that he didn't want to see any Boudreaus; he was only there to see her. Though Liam knew he was in Texas, having run into him in Wichita Falls, he didn't want to see or talk to any of the others.

Too bad he hadn't been fast enough to get out of her room before Ms. Patti muscled her way past the nurse, who Gage had sweet-talked into giving him a few minutes. There'd been no problem reading the panic on his face when he'd heard Ms. Patti's voice, his eyes darting around the room, looking for a way to escape without her notice. Unfortunately, there was only one door in or out, and she stood frozen in the doorway.

Not for long, though. She took a tentative step forward and then another.

"Gage?" There was a soft wonder in her voice.

"Hello, Ms. Patti."

"Land's sake! I can't believe it. You're here. I knew Liam

saw you when he went to Wichita Falls to see Ruby, but nobody told me you were coming to Shiloh Springs. How are you? Has life been good to you?" She smiled at him, and Ruby felt like her heart was breaking. This was the Momma Boudreau her family saw. Not the astute businesswoman who ran a successful real estate company. Not the efficient community leader who was the heartbeat of the town. Here was the woman who cared about the kids under her charge. Even if it was for a short time, Gage had been one of hers.

"I'm doing well. I've been helping Ruby out up in Wichita Falls. When I heard she'd been in an accident, I came to see if there was anything she needed. Maybe give her a ride back home."

That was the same story he'd given her when he'd snuck into her emergency room cubicle. He'd said Lucy told him she was in Shiloh Springs, but he hadn't mentioned knowing about the accident until he hit town. Which didn't explain why he'd come all the way here in the first place. They were friends, nothing more. He'd hinted in the beginning that he'd like for things to get more personal between them, but Ruby couldn't do that. For one thing, she didn't feel that way about Gage. He was a good-looking man. Even Lucy had a crush on him. But Ruby still loved Liam. She always had, and now that he was back in her life, she knew she always would. That wasn't going to change.

"You drove from Wichita Falls, five hours away, to see if Ruby needed a ride home? Young man, do I look stupid?

There's no way you could know about Ruby's accident—it only happened a couple of hours ago. And why would you think she'd need a ride home? She drove here, has her own car." Ms. Patti's eyes narrowed as she studied Gage, and though he tried to hide the fact the other woman's words affected him, Ruby had wondered the same. Ms. Patti just beat her to the punch and asked him first.

"Ms. Patti, I—"

"Save it until we get back to the ranch. You are coming home with us. We've got a lot to talk about, son."

Gage closed his eyes for a second and swallowed. "I don't think that's a good idea, ma'am. Things are going on and…"

"In this family, there are always things going on. Good thing I'm not easily shocked. Now you're here, we are going to talk. I have questions I never got answers to, and I've always needed to know where you went. CPS didn't tell us anything except your biological uncle came forward, and you were going to live with him." She took the few steps separating her and Gage and cupped his face between her hands.

"Ms. Patti, I can't talk about it." Gage shot Ruby a panicked look, silently imploring her to bail him out of this conversation. Grinning at him, she shrugged, saying, "You're on your own, bud."

"Gage Newsome, there's something you need to realize. The second you came to live at the Big House, you became one of mine. Mine and Douglas'. It doesn't matter how long you stayed with us, you are a part of this family. It broke my heart when CPS took you, but we didn't have any choice but to let you go. The least you own me are some answers."

Ruby could tell he wrestled with a myriad of emotions, his posture rigid, his face expressionless. She wondered who he was trying to fool, Ms. Patti or himself. She'd been there at the diner when he'd seen Liam. Though he'd been sarcastic and taunted Liam, she noted an almost underlying eagerness at seeing him. Hearing Ms. Patti speak about how and why Gage had left made her wonder how much that separation had affected and shaped Gage into the man who stood here today.

Gage pulled Ms. Patti into a hug with a sigh, holding onto her like she was a lifeline to his very soul. And it made her wonder if Gage was lonely.

"Alright, Ms. Patti, you win. You're right, we do need to talk, but you probably won't like what you hear. My life has been—complicated."

"Won't change how I feel, son."

The door to the cubicle swung open, and Liam started to walk in, stopping when he spotted Gage with his arms around his mother. He scowled and looked like he wanted to throttle the younger man.

"What are you doing here, Newsome?"

Gage grinned and put his arm around Ms. Patti's shoulder. Ruby rolled her eyes at his not-so-subtle maneuver. She had his number now. Figured out that he loved needling

Liam the way a brother would. It's funny how they hadn't seen each other for years and had only lived together for a short time, yet their reaction to each other was almost brotherly. But she'd bet her last dime they'd both deny it if she said anything.

"Came to talk to Ruby, and look who I ran into? Looks like it's my lucky day."

"Wish I could say the same." Liam turned away from Gage and walked over to Ruby's bedside. "The doc said you're good to go. The nurse is bringing in some papers for you to sign, and then we can spring you from this joint."

"Thank goodness!" Ruby tossed aside the thin blanket covering her and swung her legs over the side of the bed. She hadn't wanted to come to the ER in the first place, but Liam had been adamant after the accident she had to see the doctor. Especially with the bump on her head.

"Liam, you'll give Ruby a ride back to the house, right?"

"Of course, Momma."

"Good." She placed her hand on the crook of Gage's arm. "I'm taking Gage upstairs to see your father. Then we'll meet you at the Big House."

Liam frowned. "He's coming to the house?"

"Of course. We have a lot of catching up to do."

Gage swallowed, looking like he'd eaten a frog. It was almost funny, watching the man melt under the determined will of a five-foot-nothing woman.

Ruby saw the second Liam caught on to what Ms. Patti

wasn't saying. If she remembered correctly, there wasn't anybody better than Patricia Boudreau at getting the answers she wanted. Gage wasn't going to know what hit him.

"Dad said Doc Shaw thinks he'll be able to come home tomorrow. He wants him to take it easy for at least two weeks, which means no work. He's not happy about that. We will have to ride herd on him to keep him away from the job site."

"You leave your daddy to me."

"Yes, ma'am." Liam stepped aside as his mother and Gage left Ruby's room before gently pulling her into his arms. He dropped a gentle kiss atop her head and simply held her, and she wound her arms around his waist, leaning against him. Being within his embrace felt natural. Felt right, and she wished this moment could go on forever.

But after today, knowing that her dreams of finally being safe and being able to stop running had withered and died meant leaving Liam behind again. After all this time, she thought they finally believed her, that she didn't have what they wanted.

Instead, they'd lured her into a false sense of security, believing she could have a normal life.

"Ready to go?"

She nodded and smiled at the nurse who held her discharge papers. Sweeping her signature across the bottom of the pages, she accepted the small envelope of pills and listened to the instructions to take one if she had a headache or any pain. If the headache continued, come back, blah, blah, blah.

Within minutes, she was loaded into Liam's truck, and they headed toward the Boudreau ranch. He'd made sure she was securely buckled in before they'd left the hospital. Not that she'd complained. After today, she'd probably never get in a car again without making sure her seatbelt was on. It had saved her life and Nica's, too.

"Have you heard anything from Rafe? Was he able to track the SUV?

Liam shook his head. "I did talk to Rafe. Using the plate number, he found out it was stolen early this morning from Dallas. He's pretty sure they'll find it abandoned."

"I thought they'd finally decided to leave me alone. There hasn't been anybody trying to find me or harassing me for eighteen months. Why can't they leave me alone?"

"Who's after you, Ruby? I can't help you if you don't tell me everything."

"I know." She reached over and squeezed his knee. "I want to tell you. I need to tell you. Everything that's happened revolves around my mom."

"I had a feeling since you've mentioned her several times. How does she play into you disappearing?"

"Remember I told you about the agents who came to see me right before I died?" At Liam's nod, she continued. "They came to tell me my mother's family was actively looking for me. Turns out, my grandfather and uncle didn't know I existed. Mom ran away from them when she was seventeen. Made it all the way from Eastern Europe to the U.S. on her own, with very little money and a false identity."

"I knew your mom was from another country, strictly by her accent. You didn't know any of this?"

Ruby shook her head. "She never talked about her family. Remember, I was a kid. If she had trouble with her relatives, it's not like she would have discussed it with me."

"True."

She watched Liam pull the truck onto the drive leading to the Big House. The path to the house always amazed her, and she breathed in deeply, letting the scent of grass and flowers fill her. Other scents tickled her nose. And she smiled because putting them all together reminded her of the one thing she'd missed.

It smelled like home.

The drive to the house took a few minutes because the ranch was big. It was not the biggest in the state, but it was a good size for Central Texas. She blinked at all the cars, trucks, and one motorcycle parked in front.

"What's going on?"

"I've rounded up my brothers and Momma. She'll have brought Gage." And didn't he sound disgruntled about that fact, Ruby thought. "We'll figure out a way to help you, and then we'll bring you home. For good."

CHAPTER SIXTEEN

"WELL, IT LOOKS like the gang's all here."

Gage stared at all the people assembled in the living room, and Liam smirked at his frustrated expression. It had been a couple of hours since he and Ruby had left the hospital, and he'd put that time to good use. Liam sent out a group text, letting all his brothers know Gage was not only in Shiloh Springs, but he'd be at the Big House. Of course, he hadn't told all of them to show up, but he knew his brothers. They were a bunch of busybodies and even bigger gossips with curiosities to match. But only within the family. His brothers didn't tend to tell their business to anybody else in town.

Luckily, his brothers all showed up without their significant others in tow. Once they'd had a chance to interrogate...um...talk with Gage, they could decide how much or how little to share.

"It's not every day one of Momma's Lost Boys shows up out of the blue. Of course, it's not a huge surprise since I ran into you just days ago."

"I'm only here to check on Ruby," Gage shot back. He

folded his arms over his chest, his every move defiant. Liam couldn't help wondering what the other man had to hide.

"I don't care why you're here, I'm simply glad to reconnect." Ms. Patti patted his arm, her expression was filled with so much hope it almost had Liam questioning siccing his brothers on the man.

"Momma," Dane stood and walked over to wrap his arm around her shoulder, "how about we get everybody something to drink? We'll probably have that done before Liam and Gage get done glaring at each other. I doubt we'll miss anything before we're done."

She laughed, allowing Dane to steer her into the kitchen. Dane glanced over his shoulder and met Liam's gaze, giving him a nod. Dane had bought him a minute or two where he could talk without his mother hearing.

"I honestly don't care why you're in Shiloh Springs, Newsome. The one thing I do care about is that woman in the kitchen. I won't have you hurting her. If you're into something illegal or even shady, take it elsewhere. We," he gestured toward the other men gathered round, "love her and won't allow you to use her."

Gage let out a loud sigh. "Dang, Liam, you're taking all the fun outta giving you a hard time." He looked at each Boudreau before adding, "I would never do anything to hurt Ms. Patti. That woman was the one bright spot in an otherwise lousy childhood. Do you honestly think I'd have left if I'd had any choice?"

"Then why did you?" Rafe tilted his head, studying Gage.

He didn't answer right away, looking torn. Finally, he flung himself down into the armchair Dane had vacated. "I'll tell you what I can, but it'll have to wait until Ms. Patti's back. I promised her I'd tell her." Gage looked at Ruby and smiled, a soft, gentle look on his face. "This concerns you too, sugar."

"Me?"

"Yes. It wasn't a coincidence I was in Wichita Falls. Wasn't one, either, when I ran into you."

Liam stalked over and grabbed Gage by the collar, yanking him up from the chair. "Are you the one who's been after her, threatening her? Because you can say your goodbyes now since nobody will find your body when I'm through with you."

Gage pried Liam's hands off and shoved him back. "Such a hothead. No, I'm not the person who's been traumatizing Ruby. Just the opposite. I've been watching over her because I'm after the person who has been. Meeting Ruby was a bonus."

"What?" Ruby sat forward, staring at Gage. "I don't understand, so you'd better explain right now. Everything you've told me, all the help, was all a lie?"

Gage winced. "A lie of omission."

Ms. Patti and Dane walked in carrying glasses of lemonade. She stopped in the entry, noting the ratcheted-up tension permeating the room.

"What happened?"

"Nothing yet, Momma. Gage is fixing to tell us why he's really in Shiloh Springs, aren't you?" Liam shot him a look promising swift retribution if he didn't.

"Good. Now stop glaring at him like you want to punch him and sit down. Better yet, here, pass out these drinks." She shoved the tray into his hands, and he, without a word, followed her order. Not like he had a choice.

Gage leaned back, one booted foot resting on his knee. He looked relaxed and easy for the first time since he'd walked through the door. Ms. Patti sat on the oversized ottoman at the foot of the armchair where Gage sat, her smile tender.

Gage studied each person present, and Liam wondered if he was trying to gauge how much he could tell them. He had to admit his curiosity was piqued. Especially since he said he'd been watching over Ruby. It didn't sound like he'd been acting like a stalker. More like he'd been...protective.

"Everything I'm about to tell you is strictly confidential. And I cannot stress this enough. You can't tell anybody. Not your wives, your fiancées, your girlfriends, your best friends. Nobody. Anybody who's got a problem with that needs to leave."

Not a single person moved from their seats. Liam hadn't expected them to; Boudreaus knew how to keep a secret. The seriousness of Gage's expression and the solemnity of his voice made him sit up and pay attention.

"I do not sell medical equipment. I'm sure Shiloh or Ridge already checked into my background."

"I did some digging," Rafe admitted. "Of course, it was only a surface search."

Gage grinned at Rafe, pointing a finger at him. "What did your digging tell you, hoss?"

"My gut said your entire record is a lie. Oh, it's good on the surface and passes a cursory review, but it's too…I don't know…perfect."

"Good call." Gage leaned forward in his chair. "Almost everything you found is a lie. It's my cover."

"I knew it!" Shiloh punched Ridge in the shoulder. "Didn't I tell you the whole thing was a load of—" He stopped talking at the look his momma shot him.

"Cover? Why would you need a cover story?" Ruby asked the question softly.

"Because I work for the government. Specifically, the Central Intelligence Agency."

Several people started talking at once, but Liam couldn't help noticing how pale Ruby turned at Gage's words. It was almost like she'd expected his answer. Maybe she had. Pieces of things she had told him started coming together, forming a picture his brain didn't want to consider. Yet it kind of made sense in a weird way.

"People, I can't finish if you don't stop talking." The room quieted, and focus turned back to Gage. "Most of what

I do is outside the United States. I've been with the Agency since I left the Army. They recruited me," he glanced at Ms. Patti, a look of profound regret coloring his expression. "It's hard to explain this without some long, drawn-out spiel. But, when I was in middle school, the students were given what we were told were special aptitude tests. Intelligence tests. Every student took the same ones. Right after that, I came to live here."

"I remember. Did these test results have anything to do with you leaving?"

Gage leaned forward and grasped Ms. Patti's hand. "Yes. I scored off the charts in several key fields. We weren't told that these weren't standardized tests administered by the State of Texas. They were aptitude tests, that part was true, but they had nothing to do with education. I later found out that they were done randomly throughout the United States, mostly administered in small to mid-sized towns, geared toward middle school and early high school students. I was deemed a special case since I had no family."

"What about your uncle?" Liam asked.

"There was no uncle. A lot of that time is kind of a blur. It happened a long time ago. I got placed in a private school; you might call it a boarding school for kids who scored high on these tests."

"That's barbaric. And probably grossly illegal." Trust Chance to get right to the heart, Liam thought.

"Who was going to tell the U.S. government no? Certainly not an overcrowded childcare system. The right paperwork gets filed, and a kid leaves the system for a better life. It wasn't bad, don't get me wrong. I wasn't abused or mistreated. I got a great education along with specialized training. You might say the CIA recruited me before I could shave." He gave a bitter laugh. "Anyway, after two years in the Army, because that part of my background is true, they called me into active duty at the Agency. I've been working for them ever since."

"What does any of this have to do with you being friendly with Ruby? You said you've been watching over her. It almost sounds like you're a stalker—" Chance's eyes widened, and he pointed at Gage. "Unless she's a job. Is that what you're saying, Gage? Why would the CIA be interested in our Ruby?"

"Always knew you were smart, Chance. For the last three years, I've been working undercover, getting in deep with a Polish crime family. One that has major ties with organized syndicates embedded here within the U.S. I've worked my way up the ranks, and let me tell you, it hasn't been easy. This family's roots run deep, and they've got tentacles within their government. Nothing is too corrupt for this family. Murder, blackmail, gunrunning, they're deeply seated in all of it."

"Still haven't answered my question. What does any of this have to do with Ruby?" Chance stood and walked over to lean against the opening between the living room and the hall. "Corrupt families are a plague, but not uncommon, especially in countries where corruption is all too real."

"What Gage is trying to tell you is the family he's been investigating is mine. Right?" Ruby never took her eyes of Gage.

"But you're American. The CIA wouldn't have any reason to investigate you, unless…Ruby, this ties in with your death being faked, doesn't it?" Ridge ran his fingers through his hair, leaving it standing straight up on his head.

"Yes." She sent a pleading look at Liam. "Remember me telling you about the two people who came to see me? They worked for the government. They told me my mother's family was actively searching for me. They told me things about my mom I didn't know. Things like my grandfather was the head of a major crime syndicate in Europe, suspected of unspeakable crimes. Some of the things they told me—" she drew in a shaky breath. "They're monsters. My mom ran away when she was seventeen. She wanted nothing to do with them or their way of life. Made it to the States on her own. While working in New Jersey, she met my dad not long before they moved to Shiloh Springs."

"Take your time, sweetheart. I know this is rough. I never knew any of this about your mom." Ms. Patti smiled at Ruby, encouraging her to let everything out.

"I don't think anybody did. When my mom went to Poland to visit, we expected her to return. Instead, she kept calling and saying her father wasn't doing well and she needed to stay a little longer. On her last call, she talked to my dad for a long time. When I talked to her, she repeatedly told me she loved me and was sorry. I didn't know she wasn't coming back until after we hung up. Finally, my dad had to tell me she'd decided to stay in Poland."

"Oh, honey, that's awful."

"It was a long time ago, Ms. Patti. I hated that she wasn't coming home, but I think it hurt my dad more than me. See, I still had him, but he didn't have anybody. My mom was his whole world. He made sure I always knew he loved me, that I was wanted. I couldn't understand everything, I was far too young to understand. It wasn't until years later that I heard from her again."

"The letters." Liam squeezed her hand.

Ruby nodded. "My mom wrote me a letter. She didn't send it directly to me. I think she was afraid my dad might intercept it, and I wouldn't get to read it. She mailed it to Sandra Summers and asked her to make sure I got it. I got one every six months until I was twelve. Then they abruptly stopped."

Gage leaned forward, his hands resting lightly between his knees. "Any chance you still have those letters?"

She shook her head. "I did keep them. I hoarded them like they were my secret treasure. When I 'died,'" she made air quotes around the word, "I couldn't take anything with me. I never even got to go home again. The only things I had were the clothes I wore and my purse, which we managed to smuggle out of the emergency room. I always hated that I couldn't take anything personal with me."

"What did you do with the letters? Did you keep them? Burn them? Any chance they're still around?" Chance fired the questions rapid-fire at Ruby, spitting out the words like a machine gun. Liam almost chuckled at his brother's interrogation tactics. That was the prosecutor in him, wanting answers to help solve the mystery, and Chance wasn't known for being patient or tactful.

"Like I said, I kept all the letters, every one of them. They were the only link I had with my mom. They proved she loved me, even if she couldn't be with me. Those were her exact words. At six or seven years old, I didn't understand why she couldn't be with me, live in the house she'd shared with Dad and me. I felt rejected and unloved. Wondered if there was something about me that drove Mom away. Miss Sandra tried to make me understand my mother loved me and she missed me. But she couldn't be with me." Ruby rubbed absently at her forehead, wincing when she touched the lump. "No matter how many times somebody tells you they love you, it doesn't feel the same if they aren't there. I know I'm not explaining this well."

"Anybody know what happened to Ruby's stuff after— well, you know—she died?" Shiloh spoke for the first time since Ruby had started her tale. Liam knew he'd been listening intently and watching everybody's every move.

"I never really thought about it. Her dad handled everything. I don't know if he took anything with him when he moved to Oregon," Liam answered.

"Can we call him, find out what he did with her things?"

"Shiloh, my dad doesn't know I'm alive." Ruby sent him a gentle smile. "It wasn't exactly the kind of news I could share over the phone. Of course, I never planned on anybody knowing I didn't die in the accident. I should never have come back to Shiloh Springs. I've caused nothing but trouble."

"That's a load of donkey doo-doo," a female voice sounded from the doorway. Uh-oh. Liam spun around and faced his baby sister.

"Nica. I thought you were staying at the hospital, talking with Dad. He was worried about you."

"I visited with him for a while. He knows I'm fine. He fell asleep, so I left. I thought I'd come home and check on Ruby. And what do I find? A whole family meeting I wasn't invited to. Who's he?" She pointed to Gage.

"Ah, Nica, sweetheart, I'm hurt that you don't remember me."

Nica marched right up to Gage's chair, standing with her hands on her hips. Finally, a look of recognition crossed her face, and she gasped. "Gage?"

"In the flesh."

"And it's some mighty fine-looking flesh, indeed." Nica's mischievous grin had growls coming from several brothers.

"Nica!"

"Sis!"

"Girl, you better back off right now!"

"What? I'm not blind, and he's grown up mighty fine. Hey," she protested, swatting at Lucas' hands as he pulled her away from Gage's chair.

"Behave, pumpkin. Serious business going on here. You can ogle Gage later." Lucas steered his sister over to the sofa and pulled her down to sit beside him.

"Can we get back to Ruby's mom? Everything seems to lead back to her." Liam stood behind Ruby and placed his hands on her shoulders, gently squeezing them. He needed to let her know that he was there no matter what happened here. Somewhere between the time they'd left the hospital and now, Liam realized he couldn't let her go. Once they figured out who was after her, what they wanted, and the danger passed, he'd tell her the truth.

He loved her. Always had. Always would.

Admitting the truth settled something deep inside him, a restlessness he'd lived with since that day in the emergency room ten years earlier. Nothing else mattered. The lies. The danger. The years apart. The only thing that mattered was the woman seated before him. She was the center of his universe and always would be.

"Ruby, I'm sorry I have to tell you this, but your mother died a couple of years ago." Gage's voice silenced everyone in the room. Liam felt Ruby's body stiffen beneath his hands, felt the slight tremor run through her, and fought the urge to pull her into his arms and leave. He wished he could take away her pain, make everything that had happened vanish like it never happened.

"What happened to her?"

Gage's answer was abrupt and stark.

"She was murdered."

CHAPTER SEVENTEEN

"WHO?"

Ruby asked the question without any emotion, though inside, she was seething. She'd always thought her mother was somewhere in Europe, though a small part of her knew something happened when the letters stopped when she was twelve. But the reality of knowing it to be fact? Some small kernel of hope inside her died.

"We think your Uncle Piotr ordered it, though we don't have any proof. Yet," Gage qualified. "Piotr took over the family business when your grandfather died."

"Family business? Is that what we're calling it?"

"Gage, give her a break. You've broadsided her with the news. Can't she have a minute to process?" Liam moved, getting right up in Gage's face. Gage refused to back down, and Ruby stood between them, placing a hand on each man's chest.

"If you're planning on whipping out the rulers, take it outside. I can't deal with your nonsense right now."

Liam pulled her close to his side, wrapping an arm around her. "I'm sorry, sweetheart. Gage and I will table our disagreements until later, I promise."

Gage nodded. "I promise too."

Resuming her seat, she almost smiled when Liam propped his big body on the arm of the sofa, close enough she felt the warmth exuding from him. She wondered if it was because he cared or a subtle warning for Gage to keep his distance. Maybe if she kept talking, things might settle down.

"I think I need to go back to the beginning. I was visited by two people claiming to be from the government back in the day. They claimed not only my life was in danger, but the lives of everybody I cared for. My dad. Liam. All the Boudreaus. You were all mentioned by name." She held up her hand when Chance started to interrupt. "Don't. Let me get through this because it will take a while if you want me to tell you everything. Unless you want the condensed Reader's Digest version."

"Sorry."

"They showed me IDs. Said they worked for a covert branch of the government called The Guardians." She watched Gage pull out his phone and type something. He was probably texting somebody at the CIA. They'd probably never heard of the organization unless they had high clearance. She'd discovered that out the hard way. They were so far off the books they might as well be invisible.

"My uncle was looking for me. An active search showed up on the Dark Web. My mom never mentioned her family in Poland. I didn't know there were any alive until that day. They told me about my grandfather and my mother's brother, Piotr. Mother never told them she had a child. Or a husband. Until that day, it was always just Dad, Mom, and me."

"Oh, sweetheart, that had to be rough. I wish I could have helped you." Ms. Patti had tears in her eyes, and Ruby wanted to go to the other woman, let her pull her close as she'd done when Ruby was a small child. Ms. Patti's hugs always made everything feel better. But this couldn't be fixed by a hug.

"The issue wasn't just the threats against all of you. My uncle was looking for something. Is looking for something. And I don't have it, but nobody believes me."

Gage sat up straighter. "What's he looking for?"

"Something my mother supposedly gave me. Except I don't have anything. I never did. The agents who showed up told me my uncle had hired men who were headed to Shiloh Springs, determined to get whatever my mom gave me."

"Why would they think you have something?"

This time she allowed Chance's interruption. "They never said. I know they wanted to keep me alive, so we could figure out what my uncle was looking for. But my staying in Shiloh Springs put a bull's eye on me and all of you."

"Their solution was too extreme, honey. We could have kept you safe."

"Ridge, we're talking about hired assassins. They

wouldn't have cared that you were civilians; you'd be collateral damage to them. Not only were they looking for me, but the agents also said their intel mentioned y'all by name. My dad. Ms. Patti. Douglas. You were on their radar, simply because you mattered to me. The only solution to keep everyone safe meant taking me off the playing field. And to do that, I had to die." She reached for Liam's hand, needing to touch him, let him keep her grounded. Telling her ordeal was more challenging than she'd thought.

"They're the ones who arranged the accident? Snuck you out of the emergency room?" Liam voiced his question softly, and she nodded.

"We were supposed to meet after school. Like we always did. After I agreed, we decided a hit and run would be the easiest thing to stage. Doing it in a secluded place, but where we knew you'd find me."

"You were covered with blood." Liam pulled in a shaky breath. "I held you. I called nine-one-one and prayed they'd get there. How did you manage not to tell me? You were—" He broke off, unable to finish his sentence.

"The agents gave me a drug that kept me in and out of consciousness. It was like I was frozen. Everything seemed surreal. I'm still not sure what happened once we got to the emergency room. I know they had somebody at the emergency room, a doctor who helped with the records and declared me dead. He rigged the monitor to flatline, and they smuggled me out." She leaned against Liam, squeezing his biceps. "I'm so sorry. I know how much you hurt because I felt every minute of it too. I thought I was doing the right thing."

"Let's skip for a bit, Ruby. Where did these Guardians take you? I'm going to assume it was some kind of safe house?"

She nodded at Gage. "We ended up in Minnesota. Talk about culture shock. I was a seventeen-year-old girl, plucked from my life, with nobody I could talk to. Everybody thought I had died. I think I cried for weeks. Nobody let me near a cell phone, and there wasn't a landline. I think they knew I'd crack. Contact somebody. They were probably right; I would have called Liam."

"Did your uncle back off? Was the farce worth such a drastic outcome?" Nica's anger was evident. Ruby wondered if she was upset for herself or what Ruby had put her brother through?

"The short answer is no. I was isolated for about three months; the only people I saw were Daniel and Barb. One of them was always with me. If we needed food, somebody made a grocery run while the other played bodyguard. One afternoon, it started snowing. Just a light dusting at first, but it was so pretty. It was only supposed to be an inch or two, and it was cold. Barb decided to do a last-minute grocery run in case the roads became difficult. She'd been gone for about forty-five minutes when we heard a car pull up. Thinking it was her, Daniel went out to help her bring in the groceries.

Only it wasn't Barb."

She closed her eyes, vivid images of Daniel rushing inside, blood pouring from gunshot wounds in his chest and gut. He struggled to put the deadbolt and biomechanical locks in place, but his hands were covered with so much blood they kept slipping. Then, finally, he'd tossed her the keys and told her to drive far and fast away from there. She started to refuse, kneeling beside him, and trying to staunch the blood flow. Even to her untrained eye, she knew it was a futile, but she had to try.

"Barb pulled up, and they killed her before she even exited her car. Simply peppered the windshield and driver's side window with bullets. Daniel's Jeep was parked behind our cabin. I didn't know if they'd gotten around to the back, but I knew my only chance was to take it and go. Like Daniel told me to."

"It's okay, baby. Take your time." Liam squeezed her shoulder, and she felt that gentle touch right to her soul. Maybe, if she was lucky, he wouldn't hate her when he knew everything.

"I was terrified. The only two people on earth who knew I wasn't dead had just been killed. Because of me. I could hear the men talking outside. They had strict instructions not to kill me. My uncle needed me alive."

"To give him whatever he thought your mother gave you." At her nod, Gage stood and began pacing. Of course, there wasn't a lot of space, with so many Boudreaus all crowded into the living room, but he managed. "And you have no idea what it is?"

"None. I managed to climb out a window in the cabin and ran. I knew if I took the car, they'd be on me in a heartbeat. Instead, I ran into the woods enclosing the back of the cab. I took a branch to cover my footprints because of the snow. It felt like I ran for hours. I didn't know where I was. I could hear voices, the men searching for me. The snow kept falling, more than the one or two inches they predicted. I think that's the only thing that saved me."

She smiled at Nica and took the glass of water she held. "I think that's the most I've ever heard you talk in one sitting. Of course, you weren't normally around to talk to me." Nica cut her eyes at her brother and chuckled at his disgruntled expression. "Just kidding, buddy. Lighten up. We'll figure things out and keep your girl safe."

Ruby felt grateful Nica managed to cut the tension in the room. Her sharp sense of humor diffused the mounting levels of testosterone, and there was a lot of it with all these men crowded into a small space.

"You pretty much know the rest. I stayed off the grid as much as I could. Any time I thought Uncle Piotr's men found me, I moved on to another location. My only goal was keeping one step ahead. My last move was to Wichita Falls, where Liam found me."

"I'm not the one who actually found you, but that's a story for another day. You're here, and we need to come up with a plan to get your uncle to back off. Between all of us, we'll figure out a way. I promise."

She believed him. Liam had never lied to her.

"I'm going to head out. I need to talk with a couple of my contacts to see if Piotr's recently made any moves. I know we're getting close to having enough evidence to take him down, but we can't move prematurely. If we screw this up, the fallout affects a lot more than just Ruby." Gage stood and walked over to Ruby. "I promise this will end, and you'll have your life back."

"Thank you."

"Come on. I think we're done here." Liam held out his hand, and Ruby slid hers into it. The last couple of hours had taken their toll emotionally, and she could use a break.

"I think I know someplace where we can be alone. Just the two of us. No interruptions, no nosy people poking into our business." This last part was said with a glance at Nica, who stuck out her tongue at her brother.

"Momma, we'll be back in a bit."

"No worries, son. Take all the time you need."

Liam led her to the front door, and they stepped out onto the porch. She sighed, feeling like she could finally take a deep breath for the first time all day.

"I want a few minutes, just for us. How about you?"

She nodded. It sounded perfect. When he stepped off the front porch and started walking, she knew where he was leading her.

And she couldn't think of a better place to be alone with the man she loved.

CHAPTER EIGHTEEN

L EAVING EVERYONE IN the Big House, Liam led Ruby to the gazebo. The magical place wasn't a surprise to Ruby. He'd brought her here dozens of times when they'd been dating back in high school. She loved the building with its trailing flowers and ivy and had even spent a couple of sunny afternoons helping his momma plant seedlings around the gazebo's base.

"I dreamed about this place, you know. The gazebo. It was my safe place. In my dreams, we were together, spending afternoons talking and kissing. Nobody could touch us here."

"I haven't been back here since you...well, you know. I couldn't face seeing it, remembering how happy we were here." He closed his eyes, inhaling deeply. "I couldn't even smell flowers without thinking about us in the gazebo, remembering how we'd talk. Made plans for our future. Now it seems surreal, you know?"

She nodded, leaning forward, and pressed her face close to the climbing roses. She was beautiful in the dappled sunlight. One of the most stunning girls in school, now she'd matured into a woman who fueled his fantasies. He wondered if he'd ever be able to let her go again.

"Do you ever wonder what would have happened if you'd stayed? If your uncle hadn't caused all the chaos with his threats?"

She nodded, looking at him with a sad smile. "More times than you can imagine. It's a beautiful dream, our future. We'd have finished school and gotten married. Had two children, a boy who looked like you."

"And a little girl who looked like her mother."

"We'd buy a little house not far from Rafe's. A three-bedroom ranch on a quiet street, where the kids could play safely outside. You'd come home for supper and help the kids with their homework."

"Sounds perfect."

Ruby climbed the steps and peered into the depths of the well. "Remember how we used to toss coins in here, making wishes? Of course, I wanted those wishes to come true with every fiber of my being. Thinking back, I realize how silly it seems. But I knew this place was magic when I made those wishes, and they'd come true."

"If only it were that easy. Too bad life never takes the route we expect." Liam leaned against the doorjamb, watching Ruby whirl around the wishing well like she didn't have a care in the world. Sometimes he wondered why their lives had turned out so hard. Didn't they deserve a little happiness, like his brothers? Like his parents? "I'm sorry your life has been so rough. I'd change things if I could."

"I used to sit and meditate, thinking about what I'd say to you if we ever ran into each other." Her laugh filled the air, and he smiled at the sound. "It certainly wasn't anything like the real thing. When you slid into my car, I about had a heart attack."

"I have a confession. I already knew you were alive when I showed up in Wichita Falls."

"I thought—I didn't think about it at all. You were there, sitting beside me, and my whole world tilted on its axis. I was scared. Excited. Terrified. But mostly, I was happy."

"Happy?"

She nodded and sank onto the bench surrounding the inside of the gazebo. Liam flicked the switch inside the doorway. Dozens of twinkling white lights illuminated the space, and Ruby clapped her hands.

"She put in the lights! Your mom talked about how much she wanted to put Christmas lights around the roof but thought it might be too silly."

"Anything Momma wants, she gets. If Dad doesn't do it, one of us boys does."

Following his gut, he walked over and sat beside her, feeling the little zing he felt whenever he was near her. He could be standing in a crowded room, and if Ruby walked close, he'd know it instinctively. Funny how he'd missed that feeling.

"Ruby, I want to kiss you."

"Thank goodness. I was afraid I was the only one who wanted that." She shot him a cheeky grin. "You never used to ask for permission. Nope, you'd swoop in and steal a kiss, like it was the best part of your day, and you couldn't wait until we were alone."

"Kissing you *was* the best part of my day." His fingertips brushed across her cheek, the need to touch her overwhelming. He wanted something good, clean, and bright to remove all the ugliness they'd talked about earlier. Something special only shared between the two of them.

He brushed his lips across hers in a gentle kiss. Felt her lips move beneath his in response. Touching Ruby, her lips so soft, it felt like coming home.

Deepening the kiss, Liam poured everything he couldn't say into the kiss. All his want. His need. Every second of missing her, mourning her. When her lips parted beneath his, the sweetness was almost too much. Kissing Ruby was as simple as breathing. And he never wanted to stop. Her response was beautiful, knowing that she needed him as much as he needed her.

Ruby's arms twined around his neck, and his moved across her back, reveling in the feel of having the woman he loved in his arms. Where she belonged, she was it for him. Nobody else would ever be enough, not after Ruby.

Breaking their fevered kiss, she found the perfect spot to rest her head on his shoulder, snuggling into the crook of his

KATHY IVAN

neck and sighed. One of those whole-body sighs, and he felt her moving against him, sinuous as a cat. Tangling his fingers in her hair, he leaned in for another kiss, desperate for the touch and taste of her.

She was his addiction, one he never wanted to give up.

When his phone vibrated in his pocket, he wanted to toss it straight into the wishing well. Whoever it was, it better be important because their timing stank.

Looking at the caller ID, his head drooped. He had to take it; it was the construction site. They wouldn't be calling him now unless there was an emergency.

"I'm sorry, I've got to take this."

She gave him a tentative smile and leaned against him. Wrapping an arm around her waist, he pulled her close.

Answering the phone, he closed his eyes and took a deep breath, inwardly cursing the interruption. He told his foreman that he was on his way. Most days, he loved his job. Today, not so much.

"I'm sorry, baby, but I need to go. There's a problem on the job site, and nobody can handle it except me."

"I'll be fine, Liam."

He pulled her into his arms, resting his chin atop her head. Marveled at how right Ruby felt in his arms and cursed her uncle. He hoped he never met the man because he'd kill him. After losing ten years with his beloved, Liam was sure he'd find inventive ways to dispatch Piotr from the face of the earth, making sure nobody ever found the body.

"Promise me you'll stay at the Big House. I'll be back as soon as I can, but after the bullet and the car accident, I'll feel better if I know you're here and safe."

She patted his chest. "I promise."

"I don't want to leave you."

"You need to go. You're the only one who can handle things while your dad's in the hospital. I understand responsibility, Liam. I've already turned your life upside down, showing up in Shiloh Springs. I'll feel awful if I make things even worse."

Shaking his head softly, he guided her through the gazebo opening and headed back toward the house. He noted almost all the cars were gone. Guess his brothers and Gage took off after he'd left with Ruby. His mother's Escalade sat parked in front still, so she was home. Ruby's car was there, too, along with his pickup truck. He felt better knowing Ruby wouldn't be alone; his mother was here. Nica was here. Plus, Dane wasn't that far away, and he'd come running in a heartbeat if there was trouble.

"I'll be back as soon as I can. Then we can talk about this." He gestured between her body and his. "Tell me I'm not the only one feeling something special here."

"You're not alone."

"I've gotta go. Tell Momma where I am, and I'll be back as soon as I've fixed things."

"Go. The faster you leave, the faster you'll get back."

Liam laughed. "I remember you telling me your mom

used to say that."

Ruby cocked her head as if listening to a voice he couldn't hear. "You're right. I'd forgotten she used that phrase when I was little."

He dropped a quick kiss on her nose and turned, sprinting down the front steps. He didn't turn around, didn't look back, because he wouldn't have left if he did.

Things were looking up. He had his Ruby back, and everything was going to be alright.

RUBY WALKED INTO the kitchen and went straight to the sink. She needed something to do, busy work to keep her mind occupied and off the kiss with Liam.

The kiss. She'd forgotten what it felt like to kiss somebody she cared about. Feeling his lips against hers, the surge of warmth flooding her, she'd felt giddy. Almost like she was the silly schoolgirl she'd been with her first crush. Only Liam had never been a crush. He'd been her soul mate, the one man on this earth who made her feel whole. She'd walked away from him once, uprooted her life, and made the hardest decision of her life to keep him safe.

She wasn't sure she could walk away from him again.

Filling the sink with hot soapy water, she washed and rinsed the glasses from their earlier meeting. She smiled, thinking about all Liam's brothers gathered around, each ready and willing to defend her, and fight for her. Outraged at what her life after Shiloh Springs had been like. That amazed her. These strong, capable men were willing to do whatever it took to help her. She knew it was because they loved their brother. Yet they still gave their help willingly, freely. The Boudreaus were a true family in every sense of the word.

"What are you doing, sugar? I can do those."

"It's okay, Ms. Patti. I need something to keep my hands occupied. Where'd everybody go?"

"They all headed back to town. Either to work or home. Nica borrowed her dad's truck and is headed back to the hospital to spend some time with him."

"That's good. I bet she misses him when she's at school. She told me she'd be graduating soon. You must be proud of her."

"We are. Nica's worked hard to get her degrees. I shouldn't be surprised. Nica was always an overachiever. She takes after her daddy."

"Trust me, she's got a lot of her mother in there too."

Ms. Patti smiled and bumped her hip against Ruby's. "You wash, I'll dry." Working side by side felt nice. When they were done, Ms. Patti motioned to the kitchen table. "Have a seat, and let's talk. Though I'm at a loss for words after hearing what you've endured since leaving Shiloh Springs. I wish I could have been there for you."

"In a way you were."

"What do you mean?"

Ruby reached across the table and squeezed Ms. Patti's hand. How could she explain to this extraordinary woman how much she'd meant to her growing up? She'd been the mother figure in her life after her mother left. Ms. Patti had unofficially made her part of the family, first as Liam's friend and then Liam's love.

"You've always given me the strength to do anything. When I'd get into a tough place, you were always there. Maybe not physically, but you're the one who taught me how to be strong. How to stand up for what I believed in. When I hit low points, I'd think about you. About this amazing family and the love you share. I was honestly never alone because you were there. Keeping me going, keeping me strong."

Tears filled Ms. Patti's eyes. "Oh, sugar, thank you. Thank you for letting me be part of your life, even though it was never enough. I should have done more, helped you—"

"You did. Ms. Patti, don't you know how amazing you are? You took in eleven boys who'd been through some of the worst life could throw at them and made them your sons. You fought more battles, emotionally and physically, than most women ever see and came out the other side smiling. You took a sad little girl whose mother walked away, and you made her feel special. Made her realize there was still good in the world, even when everything around her was falling apart. Of course, I missed you but knowing you were here in

Shiloh Springs, taking care of your boys and Liam kept me going. It made me realize that I was strong enough to make the hard decision to keep you all safe."

Ruby stood and wrapped her arms around Ms. Patti and felt her body tremble. Her tears blurred her vision, and she gave a watery chuckle. "Look at us, a couple of watering cans."

Grabbing a paper napkin from the holder in the center of the table, Ms. Patti wiped her eyes and gave Ruby a wavering smile. "I'm glad you're home, Ruby. Trust Liam. Trust Gage. They'll figure out a way to get your uncle off your back and make it so you can come back to stay. I don't want to lose you again. I *won't* lose you again."

"I'm done running, Ms. Patti. No more secrets. No more lies. No matter what, I'm home to stay.

Ms. Patti stood and placed her hands on her hips. "Glad to hear it. Now, I'm going to head to the hospital and check on my ornery husband. He's gonna be giving the nurses fits, wanting to come home. You going to be okay here by yourself for a bit?"

"I'll be fine. Liam will be back as soon as he deals with his work situation."

"Well, Dane's around if you need anything. If he's not in the barn, he'll be at the foreman's house. His cell number is on the fridge. Don't hesitate to call him."

"I promise. Tell Douglas I'll try and get by to see him soon if they don't let him come home before I can get over there."

"I will."

Ruby watched the Boudreau matriarch grab the oversized purse she carried with her everywhere and followed her onto the porch. Then, she waved as she pulled her Escalade down the drive and headed toward town.

Looking out over the sprawling lush green lawn, she drew a deep cleansing breath and felt her spirit relax. This was it, her turning point. Ruby realized she'd already made her decision, because there wasn't any other choice she could make except one.

She wasn't going anywhere because she was finally home.

CHAPTER NINETEEN

RUBY HEARD HER cell phone ringing when she walked back into the house. She scrambled to get to it before whoever it was hung up. Digging in her purse, she pulled it free.

"Hello."

"Ruby, thank goodness! I'm so glad you answered. You have to help me."

"Lucy, what's wrong?" The panic in her partner's voice came through loud and clear. "Calm down and tell me what's wrong."

"It's Katie."

"Katie? I thought she went back home."

"Yeah, well, she never made it there. She showed up here about an hour ago. Ruby, she's a mess. Somebody did a real job on her. She's covered with cuts and bruises. She's got a black eye, and I think her nose is broken."

"What? Did she say who did it? Never mind. Call the police. Get her to the emergency room."

"She won't go. I've tried everything, and she said she wouldn't talk to anybody but you. She threatened to run away if I called the cops, and we'd never see her again. Ruby, we can't let her do that. She can't take another beating like this, it'll kill her."

With each word, Lucy's voice got more and more agitated. Lucy had never been the best at dealing with the girls when they were in crisis mode. When things were running smoothly, Lucy was the best. She could make them laugh and joke. Great with making their money stretch and getting every dollar's worth of deals, but dealing with the police? Having to see the uglier side of what their charges dealt with every day? That's when Lucy kind of fell apart.

"Lucy, you've got to stay calm. Put Katie on the phone, maybe I can convince her to talk with somebody. If she won't go to the emergency room, maybe she'll go to the clinic over on Ninth."

"She's asleep. I finally convinced her to lay down and rest. She agreed when I told her I'd call you and you'd come home. Ruby, you've gotta come home. I know you want to be there for your friend's dad, but we need you."

"Lucy, I—"

"Do you want Katie to run again? Because she will. I'm shocked she even came back here in the first place. She's hurt, scared, and you're the only one she trusts. Come home, Ruby. Please."

Could she turn her back on Katie? Or any of their girls? Situations like this were why they'd kept Haven of Hope going. For girls like Katie, who desperately needed help but didn't trust the system. She knew she didn't have any other choice.

"Alright, Lucy. I'll leave as soon as I can. Keep her calm and if you can convince her to go to the clinic, let me know, and I'll meet you there."

"Thank you! I was at my wit's end. You are a lifesaver!"

Hanging up, Ruby rifled through a couple of drawers before finding what she was looking for. She wrote a note for Liam, telling him what had happened and why she had to leave. The promise she'd made him ate at her, filling her with guilt. He'd understand, she knew, because he'd want her to do the right thing and help one of her traumatized girls.

Folding the note in half, she wrote Liam's name in big, bold letters and left it in the center of the kitchen table, sure he'd find it as soon as he got home.

With a sigh of regret, she picked up her purse and keys and headed for Wichita Falls.

WITH A HEAVY groan, Liam climbed into the cab of his truck and started toward home. He'd straightened out the so-called emergency, frustrated because it was something that a couple of phone calls could have resolved, and saved him the trip to the site.

He couldn't wait to get back to Ruby. They had a lot to

talk about, issues to resolve, but they'd work through everything. He wouldn't let her walk away, not without a fight. He might not like Gage all that much, but he had to admit, the man was trying to help Ruby get her blasted uncle off her trail. If they could figure out what her uncle thought she had and give it to him, he'd have to back off and leave her alone.

His cell phone rang. Seeing Ridge's name, he answered.

"Hey, bro."

"Liam. I think we've got a problem."

"Another one? Don't we have enough problems already?"

"Not like this. You asked me to check into Ruby and anybody associated with her. Remember, before you went to Wichita Falls to confront her? You wanted anything you could find, ammunition if you needed it. Well, I've got a bombshell, and you're not going to like it."

Liam's hands tightened around the steering wheel. His stomach clenched because he knew whatever his brother was about to tell him would change things, probably in a big way.

"Hit me."

"First, Ruby's clean. I don't have to tell you that. Despite the name changes and constant moving around, she's stayed beneath the radar and kept her nose clean. Of course, I wouldn't expect anything less from our Ruby."

"I'm not concerned about Ruby. I'm worried that some-body in her life might be dangerous. Just because her uncle hasn't sent any goons after her in almost two years, it doesn't mean he doesn't have eyeballs on her. He probably knows her every move and has for a long time. Having the threats and intimidation stop would lull her into a false sense of security. It's what I would do. Then when she's let her guard down, strike."

Ridge chuckled. "I always said you were the most devious Boudreau, which doesn't mean you're wrong. I found a lot of disturbing facts about Ruby's partner."

"Lucy?"

"Lucy Felton. Before that, she was Lucille Brent. Before that, Lacy Shelton. The list goes on. I've found at least seven different names, only going back ten years. Could be more. But that's not the scary part. There's a trail of bodies everywhere Lucy goes. I've connected at least four mysterious deaths. Lucy has a record, and she's done time, though not for murder, at least not yet. She's careful, but you can connect the dots if you know where to look."

"Have you got enough to call the cops, turn her in?" Liam slammed his foot down on the accelerator. He needed to get to Ruby. Listening to Ridge made him twitchy. Something was in the air, a grimness he couldn't explain, but every molecule of his being told him he needed to get home. Get to Ruby.

"Not yet, but I've got Destiny doing a deeper dive. Our gal will dot every I and cross every T. By the time she's done, Lucy will be lucky they don't bury her under the jail." Ridge paused, and Liam knew there was more.

"Just spit it out, bro."

"Lucy showed up in Wichita Falls a couple of months after Ruby. I don't know how she maneuvered herself into Ruby's orbit, but Lucy set up Haven of Hope and found the rental property. Somehow managed to convince Ruby to partner with her in the halfway house. It's almost like she stalked Ruby, maneuvering her into exactly where she wanted her. My instinct tells me Lucy's got her own agenda, and she's playing a long game. She wants something from Ruby, and I'm afraid any day she's going to show up in Shiloh Springs, looking to get whatever it is from Ruby."

With every word Ridge spoke, all the puzzle pieces fell into place. It made a twisted kind of logic. What better way for her Uncle Piotr to keep tabs on Ruby, and know her every move, than to set her up with a new best friend? After being on her own for so long, unable to trust anybody, finding a kindred soul must have seemed like a lifeline for Ruby.

Lucy was the perfect choice. About the same age as Ruby, she'd have been a friend. A confidant. A shoulder to lean on when the world got to be too much. Becoming her compatriot and confidant, Ruby would have eventually opened up and told Lucy all her secrets, including the location of whatever it was her Uncle Piotr wanted. It was a smart play.

Except for the serial killer part. If bodies followed in

Lucy's wake, she wouldn't have any problem eliminating Ruby if she became a liability. Like a typical mercenary, Lucy would cut and run at the first sign of trouble, and she wouldn't leave any loose ends that could lead back to her.

"I'm on my way back to the Big House. Unfortunately, I had to leave Ruby there while handling a work-related problem at the job site. Thanks for the info, Ridge."

"No problem. Oh, I talked with Rafe before I called you. He said they found the SUV that caused the accident. It was stolen. Our guys abandoned it, but not before they torched it. Probably not going to get any usable DNA for identification from it. Sorry. My guess is they're long gone, having failed to snatch up Ruby."

Pretty much what he'd suspected. She'd be safe if she stayed at the ranch. After little Jamie's kidnapping, they'd beefed up security for the entire ranch. Nobody got onto their property without somebody knowing about it.

"Thanks again. Keep me posted if Destiny finds anything more."

"I will. Kiss Ruby for me." Ridge's laugh came over the line loud and clear before he disconnected the call.

"Jerk."

Liam sped through downtown Shiloh Springs, anxiety beginning to tease at him. Knowing Ruby was safe at the ranch helped, but there was a niggling doubt in his mind, taunting him. Telling him he couldn't keep her safe. That her uncle would find her and whisk her away, and Liam would never see her again.

Get ahold of yourself. You've got to be strong and focus on keeping your girl safe. Don't invite trouble. She's at the ranch, and she's not alone. Everything's gonna be okay.

The drive seemed to take forever, but finally he pulled onto the long drive leading to the Big House. Warmth enveloped him, knowing that Ruby would be waiting for him at the end of the way, welcoming him with open arms.

Slamming on the brakes, he threw the gear into park, bounded up the steps, and pulled open the front door.

"Ruby? I'm back."

Silence greeted him. He glanced into the living room, but it was abandoned. The next stop was the kitchen. Ruby wasn't there either. He turned to leave, but a piece of paper caught his eye in the middle of the table. Spotting his name written across the folded sheet, he picked it up and started reading.

Every word was like a physical blow.

She was gone.

Ruby was headed right into the heart of danger, and he couldn't stop her.

He grabbed his cell phone and dialed Ruby's number, praying she'd answer. The call went straight to voicemail.

Racing toward his truck, he pointed it toward the road. He wasn't sure how much of a head start Ruby had, but he wouldn't give up. Wouldn't stop, wouldn't hesitate, until he found her.

He pointed the truck toward Wichita Falls. Again. Only this time, he had to stop a killer before she murdered the only woman he'd ever loved.

CHAPTER TWENTY

"**B**RIAN, I NEED a favor."

"Unless it's an emergency, it's gonna have to wait. I'm in the middle of something—"

"It's an emergency. Ruby's life's on the line."

"Tell me."

Liam slammed his foot down on the accelerator, inching the speedometer closer to a hundred miles an hour. He wished he could teleport because every minute it took to get to Ruby was a minute too long. He cursed himself for not realizing what a chump he'd been for believing Lucy.

"Lucy's got Ruby, and she will kill her unless she gets what she wants. I'm on my way, but still at least an hour out. How fast can you get to their house?"

"Maybe ten minutes. I'm heading there now. Lucky for you I'm already in my car. Tell me what's going on. The last I heard from your mother, you and Ruby were all lovey-dovey, and she expected to hear wedding bells soon. How did Ruby end up back in Wichita Falls without you? And I thought Lucy was her friend. They manage their halfway house place together."

Liam slammed his fist against the steering wheel, spotting big orange road construction signs ahead. Traffic began slowing, cars jockeying for position, trying to move to the far right lane so they could exit the highway, hoping to make better time on the service road. With a glance, he saw the service road was as tangled with traffic as the highway, and decided to stick to his current route, praying the construction zone was a large one.

"Lucy's been playing a long game, working her way into Ruby's life. It's all been a ploy to get Ruby to trust her. She's not Ruby's friend, she works for Ruby's uncle, Piotr Stanislav."

He heard Brian spew out a string of curses. Guess Uncle Piotr's name was one Brian recognized. Of course, being the current head of one of the most prominent organized crime families in Europe, it wasn't like he kept a low profile.

"That's cold. She's been playing with Ruby's life for a year and a half? Means Piotr thinks Ruby knows something that he needs to keep quiet, or she's got something that'll cause him problems."

"Option number two. Piotr thinks Ruby has information her mother smuggled out when she ran. Supposedly a list of clients who purchased black-market arms smuggled by the Stanislav family. Enough illegal arms to overthrow a small country. There's talk of a list of high-placed officials in several countries who Piotr and company have been blackmailing, along with the evidence of the incriminating material for said blackmail. Some of these officials are higher-ups in countries that are pro-American friendly governments. This kind of information could cause upheavals that we haven't seen in our lifetimes. Is that enough to get your backside moving faster, man, because I just ran into a construction backup, and I'm stuck."

"I'm driving as fast as I can. If Ruby has a list containing information like that, wouldn't she have turned it over and made her life easier? She could have saved herself ten years of heartache and lies."

"That's part of the problem. Ruby doesn't have what they're looking for. She never had it. When her mother left, when Ruby was little, she didn't leave anything with Ruby. No lists, no papers. If it was hidden away in some of her mom's stuff, it's long gone because Ruby's dad didn't keep anything that belonged to her mother."

Liam's fist hit the horn, blaring out the sound in frustration. Moving at a snail's pace wasn't helping. He needed to get to Ruby. That anxious feeling in the pit of his stomach urged him to move, find the woman he loved because there was so much she didn't know. She was flying blind, not knowing that Lucy was a villain, one who had no compunction about leaving a trail of bodies in her wake. Shiloh and Destiny's research had turned up at least four suspicious deaths tied to Lucy. Even her name was a lie, just like everything else about the woman who'd befriended Ruby and made her feel like she was safe. His hands tightened around the steering wheel, wishing it was Lucy's neck.

"Her uncle must have a reason for thinking Ruby has this damaging evidence. Seems odd he didn't start searching for her until she was in high school. If he suspected Ruby's mom of having enough evidence to take down him and his entire organization, why wait?"

"From what we've figured out, Ruby's mom never told anybody that she had a child. Or a husband. She manufactured an entire other life, planting false evidence to lead them on a wild goose chase. Even the fact that Ruby was born at home helped because there were no hospital records."

"I'm confused. Let's see if I can get this straight. Ruby's mom went back to Poland why?"

"Supposedly her father was sick, on his deathbed. Even though she'd left Poland far behind, she kept her eyes and ears open. It was the only way she could stay one step ahead of her father and brother. She got information that her father was dying. Made the mistake of going back to say her final goodbye."

"That wasn't a smart move. Emotions trip you up every time." Brian's voice had an odd edge to it, like he'd been there, done that, one time too many. Liam wondered if the other man was thinking about his emotional attachment to Ms. Patti. Of course, anybody who'd met his momma loved her. Brian was no exception.

"We don't know if it was a deliberate trap to get her

there or whether the old man actually was ill. We do know her mother never returned to the U.S."

He slammed his foot on the brakes when the idiot in front of him swerved to the right lane, couldn't make it cleanly, and pulled back into the lane in front of Liam.

Where'd he get his driver's license, a Cracker Jack box?

"Do you think Ruby's mom smuggled out evidence against the Stanislav family? Or was this an elaborate smokescreen to draw her out and maybe bring her back into the familial fold?"

"There are a lot easier ways to reconnect with family. Piotr could have simply called her and made a connection. Gage mentioned Piotr's not allowed onto U.S. soil, but Ruby wouldn't have known that, especially at seventeen. Ruby has the biggest heart. She would have welcomed additional family with open arms, especially if they could give her information on her mother."

"The mother who abandoned her," Brian added sarcastically. Liam forgot the man didn't know about the letters from Ruby's mom. He quickly filled him in. Told him about how they'd abruptly stopped. And the fact that Gage told Ruby her mother had been murdered by her brother, Piotr.

"How would Gage know that?" Brian demanded.

"I'm not at liberty to tell you that." He couldn't, he'd given Gage his word not to reveal he worked for the CIA.

"I knew it. He's a government man. Not FBI. I'd know if he was working in my sandbox."

"Don't ask me any questions because I can't tell you anything."

There was a long moment where neither man said anything before Brian replied. "Understood. Back to Ruby because I'm about a minute out. What's the situation?"

The traffic had finally started moving, and Liam threaded his way between cars, finally able to accelerate well past the posted speed limit. The sense of urgency rode him, every second seeming like an eternity. Talking to Brian kept him distracted enough that he wasn't focused on what Lucy might be doing to Ruby. But it was in his mind, forcing him to keep moving forward.

He'd lost her once to death. Barely survived the grief and despair of that loss. To lose her again? This time, he knew he couldn't live without her. A world without Ruby in it wasn't a world worth living in.

"Lucy contacted Ruby, claiming there was an emergency. One of the women they'd been helping showed up, beaten half to death. Said she refused to talk to anybody but Ruby. Claimed if she didn't see Ruby, talk to her face-to-face, she'd kill herself."

"That doesn't make sense. Lucy's perfectly capable of dealing with the women. More so from what I've gleaned. She has a psychology degree—Ruby's more of the hands-on person. Even the house is in Lucy's name. Though truthfully, Ruby's the heart and soul of the place. Yeah, I did my homework. After I found out your connection to Ruby, I checked her out before I gave you that picture. Don't shoot the messenger, dude, because I wasn't about to pull somebody back into your orbit that might be dangerous to you or any of the Boudreaus."

"It's a trap. I wasn't at the Big House when she got the call. I'd gone to the job site to handle an emergency. By the time I got back, she'd already left for Wichita Falls and left me a note. A stinking note. I'm at least a couple of hours behind her. So, she's already there."

"Okay, stay calm. I'm here. I am parking a couple of houses down the street, so hopefully nobody spots me. It shouldn't be an issue because Ruby's never met me, and I've only met Lucy once in passing."

"Brian, be careful."

"I'm going to hang up, I need to concentrate. Going around the back and see if I can see anything. Don't call me. I'll call you when I've got anything."

Liam drew in a deep breath and let it out slowly. He hated being useless.

"Thanks. Just—keep her safe."

"I will." Brian's promise was the last thing he heard because he'd hung up.

"Please, please, let her be safe." He uttered the mantra over and over softly as he sped down the highway, praying he'd get there on time.

He had to save Ruby.

CHAPTER TWENTY-ONE

RUBY PRIED HER eyes open, wincing against the bright light overhead. Mouth dry, she tried to swallow, tasting a strange chemical taste on the back of her tongue. A bit of drool rolled out of the corner of her mouth, and she reached to wipe it off. She felt groggy and disoriented, an unusual weakness permeating her body.

Her arm didn't move, felt like it weighed hundreds of pounds. Nausea roiled deep in her belly. Lifting her head, she looked around, hoping to recognize something. Anything.

Bits and pieces were coming back, and with the memories the realization she'd been played for a fool.

"Looks like you're finally awake. I was afraid I'd given you too much."

"Too much what?"

Lucy moved to stand over Ruby's prone body, a smirk pulling her lips up in a rictus of mirth. "Oh, a little bit of this, and a smidge of that. Just something to make you go nighty-night. I had a few things to take care of before having our private party."

"Where's Katie?" She remembered Lucy's frantic call and her imploring cries that Katie had come back. Her tearful description of Katie's condition, saying her boyfriend had caught up with her and beaten the stuffing out of her. When Ruby insisted she take Katie to the hospital and call the police, Lucy swore she would, but Katie threatened to leave again if she couldn't talk to Ruby. Lucy's tearful plea had forced Ruby to do what she'd promised Liam she wouldn't.

"As far as I know, Katie's home in the loving embrace of her doting mother." Lucy pulled on the rope that secured Ruby to the headboard, making sure it was good and tight. Ruby could attest it was, the rough coil around her wrist practically cut off her circulation.

"Why are you doing this, Lucy? We're friends."

"And you're a fool. What you are is a job. A long-term, tiring, monotonous job. Such a do-gooder. You are always helping the underdog. Did you ever once consider all the good you could do with the money your family offered? Just give them the ring, and none of this would be necessary."

She tugged hard on the length of rope encircling Ruby's foot, and she bit back a scream. What was Lucy talking about? She didn't have a ring. Rarely wore jewelry. It hadn't seemed worth it, constantly moving from place to place. It was easier not to have any than try to keep track of unimportant things.

She needed to keep Lucy talking. Find out what she wanted and pray somebody came. The house sounded empty, but undoubtedly one of the girls would be home soon.

"What ring, Lucy? I don't have a ring."

"You'd better hope you have that ring, sister, because it's the only thing keeping you breathing. Your uncle wants the ring back, and he's paying me buckets of money to get it for him. Play nice, and you'll walk away with your skin intact." Reaching behind her, Lucy pulled a hunting knife from her waistband and flashed it before Ruby's face. Light glinted off the blade, casting prisms of color against the ceiling.

"Lucy, I swear I don't have any ring. But if you tell me what it looks like, maybe I can remember if I've seen it."

She gasped when the back of the blade slid against her bare arm. Lucy simply smiled and flicked the blade under the edge of her sleeve. A quick flick of her wrist, and it split to the shoulder seam. Ruby bit back her whimper.

"Ruby, as much as I'd love to toy with you, spend days seeing how much pain you can tolerate, I don't have that luxury. I'm sure your honey-bunny knows you've left that stinking backwater town you used to call home. Do you think he's already on his way? Think he's going to show up light a white knight, riding to the rescue of the helpless princess?"

"You're nuts."

Lucy's laugh was high-pitched, the sound causing goose-bumps to pop along Ruby's skin. A maniacal glint shone in Lucy's eyes as she bent close to Ruby, whispering in her ear.

"Not the first time I've heard that, princess. I've had head shrinkers study me, but nobody could keep me contained for long. I'm good at faking sanity. That's the easy part. The hard part? Not letting anybody see how much I enjoy a little torture—watching somebody squirm, knowing that I hold their fate in my hands. It's a powerful rush. Can you feel it, Ruby? Feel the adrenaline surging through your blood-stream? Feel the heightened tension, hear the ticking clock?"

"Lucy, please." Ruby tugged at her restraints but felt no give. Kicking her legs was useless; the bonds were too tight. The knife moved closer as Lucy leaned over her bound body, toying with a lock of Ruby's hair. Lifting the blade, she ran it across the lock, shaving off an inch and sprinkling it across Ruby's chest.

"Tell me where you've hidden the ring, Ruby. Tick, tick, tick. Time's running out. Your Uncle Piotr's pulling the plug on my involvement, so time's almost up. If I don't produce that ring, give him the information, I'm toast." She leaned in close, her face mere inches from Ruby's. "And if it comes down to you or me? Bet you can guess who's coming out on top."

"This ring, the one you're looking for? Maybe I do know where it is." Ruby threw out the lie, hoping Lucy would take the bait. She was winging it, hoping Liam found her note and brought the calvary. Except he wouldn't know anything was wrong other than one of Ruby's girls needed help. He trusted her and knew she cared about her work at their private halfway house. Closing her eyes, she realized she might not have rescue coming. She was on her own and needed to come up with a plan, because she wasn't going to simply lay down and die. There was far too much to live for.

"Stop blowing smoke, I'm not buying it. You're lying, and I've had enough." Lucy swung the blade high, and Ruby screamed when she felt it sink into her forearm. She waited for the pain and blinked when she realized there wasn't any.

"That's my final warning, sister. The next time, I'll use the sharp edge, and the blood will flow. Where is the ring?"

"That's why I asked you to describe the ring," Ruby shouted her answer to Lucy, allowing fear and frustration to pepper her words. "There's more than one ring. Unfortunately, I can't tell you where it is until I know which one you're looking for."

Lucy studied her face closely, and Ruby prayed she couldn't read the lie. Although she'd gotten better about lying when she'd been on the run, she'd gotten out of the habit. Now she wished she'd kept up with her deception.

"This is ridiculous. Your freaking mother left you more than one ring? Do you think I'm stupid or something?"

"No. My mother left me a ring and my father a ring. Two rings."

"Argh! Piotr didn't say anything about two." She narrowed her eyes and watched Ruby closely.

Ruby held herself completely still.

Please believe me. Please, please believe me.

"Lucy, I don't have the rings here. You know that, or you'd have already found them. Because you've searched, right?"

Lucy nodded, her fingers toying with the knife. She slid one finger against the sharp blade and studied the drop of blood that pooled on her fingertip. "I've torn this house apart looking for the ring. Singular. Where are they, Ruby? No more evasions. No more lies. I have places to go, people to see." The last was added in a singsong voice, each word higher than the previous one.

"I have to take you to them."

"Nuh-uh. Tell me, and I'll go and get them. I'm not untying you. The first chance you get, you're going to try and overpower me and run." Lucy giggled, and the sound sent an icy chill down Ruby's spine. Whatever sanity Lucy might've had before, it was long gone.

"Let's make a deal, Lucy."

Lucy's eyes narrowed. "What kind of deal?"

You want the rings. The money my Uncle Piotr offered, right?" At Lucy's nod, she continued. "Well, I want to live. If I take you to the rings and give them to you, give me your word that you'll let me go. I'll disappear again. I'm very good at vanishing. Uncle Piotr and the family looked for me for close to ten years, and I'm still not sitting in their dungeon in Poland, am I?"

"I found you easily enough," Lucy scoffed.

"But you want things over with. We can make that happen. You get your money and don't have to babysit me anymore. I get to stay alive. Sounds like a win-win."

"I need to think. I'm not sure because if you're lying..."

"You've got a knife to my throat. Trust me, it's not in my best interest to lie. Come on, Lucy, don't you want a chance to stick it to the man? Uncle Piotr's got more money than he can ever spend. You can make him pay through the nose to get those rings back. I get my freedom. Don't have to pretend that I'll be the perfect little wife and mommy to my high school sweetheart."

A slow smile curved Lucy's lips, and she flipped the knife end-over-end, catching it expertly. "That's the first intelligent thing you've said all day. I couldn't picture you settling down with Mr. Perfect. Liam Boudreau wouldn't understand the real you, Ruby. You've always been footloose. I can't see you settling down and spitting out kiddos."

"I thought about it for a minute, I'll admit." Ruby shot Lucy a grin and fervently hoped she bought the flat-out lie she'd just uttered. She'd give everything to be with Liam. To spend every day with him, loving him. Having his children was her fervent wish and dream. But she had to convince Lucy she meant all the bald-faced lies she told her.

"Tell me where the rings are first."

"They're in a locker. I got one when I decided to relocate to Wichita Falls. There's not much in it other than the few things I don't want to lose. I've had to pick up and run, often leaving everything behind except the clothes on my back and what I carried in my purse. I learned to keep the important stuff locked away. Do you have any idea how many times I've been robbed? Trust me, when you sleep on the streets, in alleyways, you're fair game to anybody bigger than you."

"Where? I'm tired of you stalling and playing games with me. Do you want your deal? I want the location of the locker."

Ruby drew in a jagged breath and gave Lucy an answer she hoped she'd believe.

"YMCA on Birmingham Street."

Lucy closed her eyes and cursed. "Seriously?"

"Think about it. It's a secure place, nobody would think to look there. You can rent a small locker for less than ten bucks a month. I've done it in city after city. There's always somebody around at the Y to prevent criminals from strolling in and breaking into the lockers."

Lucy reached forward with the knife and slid it beneath the rope holding her right ankle to the footboard. It took a couple of tries, but the rope split, freeing her. She repeated her action on the other foot.

"If you're screwing with me, sister, there will be no second chance. I'll be long gone before they ever find your body."

"I want this over with. I'm sick of constantly looking over my shoulder. Give the rings to Piotr and tell him I'm no problem for him. I'll go underground, and he'll never hear from me."

Within a minute, the bonds on her wrists were slit, and Ruby rubbed her wrists, feeling the pins and needles sensation as the circulation returned to her limbs.

"Let's go. You drive."

Ruby started toward the bedroom door, but something, some movement, caught her attention. Cutting her eyes toward the window, she noticed a strange man crouched down, his head barely clearing the sill. He raised a finger to his lips in a shushing motion. Then he disappeared.

Who was he? Why had he been there? Then, finally, she realized it didn't matter. For the first time since this whole debacle started, she had hope she might get out of things alive.

And back with Liam.

CHAPTER TWENTY-TWO

L IAM HAD CROSSED the city limits into Wichita Falls and headed toward Ruby's house. He hadn't heard anything from Brian, and that worried him. Too much time had passed since he'd spoken with him. Had he located Ruby?

When his phone rang, he didn't bother looking at the caller ID, answered it before the second ring.

"Hello?"

"It's me. I found Ruby."

The constriction in Liam's chest eased, and he took his first free breath since he'd found out Ruby had left Shiloh Springs.

"Is she okay?"

"She's alive, and right now, unhurt. It's a long story, and we don't have time to go into that now. Ruby and Lucy are on their way to the YMCA on Birmingham." Brian gave him the address as well as the cross street. Liam had a pretty good idea where it was since Birmingham was a busy street.

"Why are they going to the Y?"

"Because Ruby told Lucy she kept a locker there, and that's where the ring is that Ruby's uncle is looking for."

"A ring? All this is about some stupid ring?"

"Yep." Brian chuckled, and Liam wondered what the man found funny. There was nothing humorous about this entire situation. "Lemme tell you, dude, your girl is a pretty darn good liar. She had Lucy buying every word coming out of her mouth. Claimed there were two rings. One her mother left her, and one dear old mom gave to Dad."

"That's not right. Ruby doesn't have anything from her mother. Certainly not a ring. She'd have told me."

"Like I said, she's a good liar. Lucy bought it. They're on their way to the Y to get the rings from a locker Ruby said she rented when she moved to Wichita Falls. As lies go, that's a smart one. There is no way to check out the fact, and there are always people around the Y, so Lucy has to be careful what she says and especially what she does."

"How close are you?"

"I've got eyes on them right now. I was outside the bedroom window the whole time, ready to make my move if needed. But, because there was no immediate danger, I let them talk and figured the longer Ruby could stall Lucy, the closer you'd be." Brian paused for a second, which ratcheted up Liam's pulse rate. He didn't like silence, not in instances like this one. "I'm behind them on Birmingham. Probably two minutes until we get to the YMCA building. Please tell me you're close."

"Maybe ten minutes. Fifteen tops. Think you can stall 'em?"

"I can try. Ruby saw me as they were leaving. She'll recognize me and hopefully figure out I'm one of the good guys. Lucy, I've met once. Whether she'll remember, that's touch and go. I'll step in if I have to. But, brother, drive faster!"

Liam smashed the accelerator down, blowing past a stop sign. If any cops saw him, let them follow, he could use the backup. He sped toward Birmingham and made a right, tires squealing as he took the corner.

He pulled into the parking lot and slammed the car into park, quickly heading toward the door. Throwing the glass door open, he stopped after walking through, getting his bearings. Ruby and Lucy were nowhere in sight. He didn't spot Brian, either.

He strode toward an employee who held a broom and a dustpan, a slightly glazed expression on his face. The guy was young and skinny, with long, greasy hair spilling over his shoulders. A half-empty pack of cigarettes filled the front pocket of his shirt, and the body odor coming off him was enough to fell an elephant. In a place that boasted a total gym and showers, he bit back the urge to tell the guy to take advantage of the amenities.

"Where are the rented lockers?"

He pointed before scratching at his pimple-covered chin. "Pretty busy area tonight. You're like the third person to ask me that in the last five minutes."

"You have no idea." Liam sprinted past the puzzled kid, heading toward where he'd pointed. Unfortunately, the lockers were against the wall, and he found himself facing a disaster.

Lucy held a sharp knife to Ruby's neck, tiny droplets of blood trailing from a small nick. Brian stood facing the women, his hands raised to shoulder height. Obviously, things had gone straight into the toilet, otherwise, Brian wouldn't have shown himself before Liam got there.

"I told you, back off. I don't care who you are; you will not stop me from getting what I've earned." Lucy shifted her stance, the knife never leaving Ruby's throat. Blood pounded in Liam's ears as he watched the deranged darling keep her focus on Brian. He had to admit, the FBI agent was doing a good job keeping Lucy off balance.

"Lady, I don't know what your problem is, but I can't let you hold a knife on anybody. Are you nuts? The cops will lock you up and throw away the key for a stunt like this. Let's all chill. What can I do to make this whole thing go away? You want money? I can give you everything I've got on me. Shoot, there's an ATM over there." Brian pointed. "I'll take out the max and give it to you. Just let the crying lady go."

"I don't want your stinking money. Leave. I'm not telling you again. This is between Ruby and me. She lied to me, and now she will pay the price. If I can't get what I was promised, we'll simply have to improvise." Keeping the knife at Ruby's throat, she twisted her other hand in Ruby's hair, yanking her head back at an almost impossible angle.

"Wait. Don't hurt her. Please." Liam stepped forward, drawing Lucy's attention away from Brian and onto him. "I know who you are, Lucy. Felton's not your real name. You've had a rather colorful past. Guess what? I don't care. You let Ruby go, and we'll let you walk out of here. No cops. No feds. I've read your file, and I know exactly how dangerous you are. I don't want any trouble. Just let Ruby go, and we'll all walk out of this without anybody getting hurt."

Lucy's laugh was deep and ugly. "You haven't got a clue who you're dealing with, Liam Boudreau. Nobody does. I've spent the last eighteen months living with little Miss Goody Two-Shoes because I knew she'd eventually lead me to Piotr's ring."

"A ring? That's what you've been looking for?"

"Like you don't know. I bet you've been chasing after Ruby, hoping to get that ring. Her uncle offered me half a million dollars upon finding it and another half-million when I deliver. Do you seriously think I'm walking away from that kind of haul?"

Liam watched Brian take a small step closer to the two women. Turning his focus back to Lucy, he watched Ruby ball her hands into fists. Uh oh.

"What's so important about this ring, Lucy? That's a lot of money for one piece of jewelry."

"Don't know. Don't care. This one," Lucy yanked on Ruby's hair again, "told me she had two rings her mother gave her locked up right here at the YMCA. Only she lied."

"Did she? Are you sure about that, Lucy? Because they were here when I opened the locker an hour ago." Liam told the lie easily, needing to get Lucy's attention off Ruby and onto him. If he could get her distracted and make her make a mistake, Brian might be able to get that knife out of Lucy's hand. "Unless you're willing to work with me, you'll never see the rings or the money."

"Give them to me." Lucy's scream was tinged with hysteria. "I've busted my backside, playing Ruby's best friend. Trying to get her to lower her guard, trust me with all her secrets. But she's as wound up as tight as a virgin on her wedding night."

"I'll take you to the rings, Lucy. We don't need Ruby anymore. Why do you think I've been sniffing around her? Certainly not because she was my high school sweetie. Women are a dime a dozen. I knew there was more to Ruby disappearing than her father told me. Figured she'd show up eventually. I can't believe she was stupid enough to come back to Texas." Liam glanced at Ruby and could easily read the fear in her eyes.

"You couldn't have known. It took me six months to even get a whiff of her in that backwater town."

"Guess you didn't have as good a hacker as I do. The minute Ruby stepped foot in Texas, I knew about it." He gave a scoffing laugh. "Ruby, Ruby. You should have stayed out of my state. I wouldn't have looked for you. Well, not until I heard about your uncle's bounty. Did you know he's willing to pay two million dollars to anybody who will bring you to him alive and kicking? Toss in the ring, and I will be set for life."

"No! That's my money. You can't have it, and you can't have her!"

Liam knew he'd made a mistake when Lucy pulled the knife away from Ruby's throat and raised it high, ready to plunge it into the woman he loved.

"No!"

Before he could move, Brian raced forward, thrusting his body in front of Ruby's, as a human shield. Liam watched as Lucy thrust the knife into Brian's shoulder, blood pouring from the wound.

Liam tackled Lucy, struggling with the manic woman. She fought and kicked, throwing punches. Blows landed, but he didn't feel them, too focused on keeping her from hurting anybody else.

"Liam!" Ruby screamed, kneeling beside Brian, her hands covering the wound in his shoulder. Blood seeped between her fingers, staining the carpet beneath her knees.

The sound of pounding feet followed by the uniformed officers seemed like a miracle. Before he could blink, Lucy was in handcuffs, and an officer radioed for an ambulance to take care of Brian.

He pulled Ruby into his arms, holding her tight. The terror of seeing her in the grip of a madwoman haunted him, and he'd felt helpless. She'd have slit Ruby's throat if he'd tried to attack. He didn't doubt that. But now, Lucy was in custody and couldn't hurt anybody.

EMTs came around the corner and immediately started treating Brian, who cursed as they probed and prodded the wound. He was still bleeding profusely, and they scooped him up, placed him on the gurney, and rushed away.

"Is he going to be okay?"

"He'd better be. I owe the man. He saved your life."

"Folks, I need you to tell me what happened here tonight. We got a nine-one-one call from the janitor that something strange was going on, and that a crazy woman held a knife to another lady's throat."

"That pretty much sums it up. Look, we'll be happy to give you a statement, but we need to get to the hospital to make sure our friend's okay. The alleged crazy woman stabbed him."

"The EMTs said it looked like an artery got nicked. Chances are he's going straight to surgery as soon as he hits the hospital. We'll have them give us a call and update us as soon as we know something. In the meantime, why don't you come with us and let's get everything straightened out?"

Liam and Ruby followed the officer out to a waiting squad car and climbed in the back. He wrapped his arms around Ruby, pulling her close.

"It's over, baby. Between what Lucy said in front of witnesses, one of whom is an FBI agent, your Uncle Piotr should back off. You can come home."

"Home. Yes, Liam, let's go home."

CHAPTER TWENTY-THREE

RUBY SMOOTHED DOWN the hem of her skirt, her palms sweaty. She couldn't remember being this nervous in a long time. It had been two days since everything went down in Wichita Falls. Lucy was in jail, facing so many charges she'd probably never see the outside of a prison cell again. Secretly, she thought Lucy would go for an insanity plea. She'd probably get it, too, because Lucy was stone-cold crazy.

Unfortunately, there was no way to prove her Uncle Piotr was responsible for everything that happened. She doubted he'd ever pay for killing her mother or hiring assassins to kidnap her and bring her to Poland. But at least she didn't have to hide anymore. Gage was reporting everything they knew to the CIA. Ruby didn't care what they did with that information, as long as they left her and Liam out of it.

"You ready, sweetheart?"

Liam brushed his knuckles against her cheek, and her skin tingled beneath his touch. She couldn't believe he'd come for her. Couldn't believe he'd sent Brian to watch over her and keep her safe until he got there.

Brian had paid the price for it, too. They'd rushed him into surgery for the knife wound. Unfortunately, Lucy's aim did nick an artery. After they'd finished giving their statements to the Wichita Falls police, she and Liam spent the rest of the evening at the hospital, waiting for Brian to get out of surgery.

The surgeon assured them Brian would make a full recovery. She didn't doubt that for a second because the following day, Ms. Patti showed up, and Ruby had the feeling Brian was about to be spoiled by the champion of all mommas. He deserved it. He'd put his life on the line, and she'd never forget his bravery. Lucy had been aiming for Ruby's heart, her wail a bloodcurdling screech Ruby still heard in her nightmares.

Talking to her dad had been harder and more complicated than she'd thought. He'd been hurt, not only that she'd lied to him, but because she hadn't trusted him. They'd talked for hours, and she finally convinced him to forgive her. A promise to come to Oregon for an extended visit had helped. They had a long way to go to rebuild their relationship, but she'd do whatever it took because she wanted her dad back in her life.

"I'm ready."

She and Liam had flown to Florida that morning, rented a car, and drove to the Summers' home. Ben Summers had given them directions and warned them that Sandra was weak from her last chemo treatment, but she'd rallied when he'd told her Ruby was coming.

Liam rapped on the condo's front door, and Ben Summers opened it with a massive smile. He ushered them inside, directing them onto the sprawling outdoor pool and spa overlooking the patio. Sandra sat at a table on the balcony, and her face lit when she spotted Ruby. She started to stand, and Ruby rushed forward, stopping her.

"It's so good to see you, Miss Sandra. I've missed you." Ruby carefully pulled the older woman into a gentle hug. Tears welled in her eyes because the vibrant woman she remembered had aged. Cancer had taken away the vital and lively woman she remembered, though the smile she gave Ruby was as full of love as always.

"Oh, Ruby, girl. Is it really you?"

"It's her, Mother." Ben Summers moved to stand behind his wife, placing a hand on her shoulder. "It nearly broke her heart when they told us you…"

"Died? I'm sorry about the deception. It's a long and complicated story we can talk about later. I need to talk to Miss Sandra about my mother, if that's alright?"

Ben nodded and gestured to a chair. "My Sandra, she loved your mother."

"My mom loved her too." Turning to Miss Sandra, Ruby took her frail hand between hers and leaned in closer. "Miss Sandra, remember all those letters my mom sent me?"

"Of course. One every six months, like clockwork. I

remember how much you looked forward to each one. So did I."

"They were my lifeline with Mom. She told me how much she loved me. That she wished she could come home. I missed her so much."

"She missed you too. Her letters were filled with questions about you, how you were doing in school, and were you making friends." Sandra glanced at Liam. "She even asked about young Liam."

"Mom wrote you letters too?"

"Of course she did. I got one every six months, just like you. She'd always enclosed your letter with mine, so nobody saw the one addressed to you. She was very careful that her family didn't know about the letters. She had to sneak them out to a friend, who mailed them for her. That's how I wrote back: I mailed it to her friend, and they'd make sure your mom got it."

Sandra struggled to stand and waved Ruby back into her seat when she stood. "I want to show you something."

Using a bright blue aluminum cane, she made her way across the balcony and into the living room, picked up a small wooden box, and brought it back out to the patio.

"Your mom sent me this. Isn't it beautiful?"

It was a lovely piece, with decorative carvings all over the lid and outside. Made of hard dark wood, the artist had taken exquisite care with each panel, each carving dramatic and beautiful.

"It's lovely." Ruby handed it back to Sandra.

"The box was a gift for me, but what's inside was always meant for you. Your mother made me promise I'd hold onto it. Keep it safe. I was to give it to you on your eighteenth birthday."

"For me?"

Sandra nodded. "Open it."

Ruby took a deep breath and lifted the lid. Inside, atop a deep red velvet lining, sat a ring. It was a man's ring with a family crest on the stone. She immediately recognized it as her mother's family crest. Knew what it looked like, because she and Liam had gone online and looked for any information concerning the Stanislav family. It matched her mother's golden pendant; one she'd worn on a long chain she kept tucked inside her blouses. The emblem matched the one on the ring.

"Liam?"

"I know, sweetheart."

Picking up the ring, she turned it over and looked at the inside, not sure what she expected. No inscription. No invisible magic writing suddenly appeared. It was simply a ring. Nothing more. Nothing that people should have lost their lives over it.

"I kept my word to your mother. I held onto it. But then you died, and I didn't know what to do with it. She didn't say anything about giving it to your father, though I was tempted to do that. It was a very confusing time. Things got rough for me not long after that, and I hate to admit it, but I forgot about the ring."

"Sandra was diagnosed with cancer. Between the hospitals, nursing home stays, treatments, and chemotherapy, many things fell through the cracks." Ben's gaze met Ruby's, and she nodded her understanding. "We ended up walking away from the farm and moving here because there was a specialist who works with the type of cancer Sandra has."

"I understand, Mr. Summers. There's no blame here. I simply wanted to talk with somebody who knew and loved my mom. Miss Sandra was the first person I thought about."

"Here, Ruby." She pressed the box into Ruby's hands. "Take this. Your mother always meant for you to have it."

"But the box is yours."

"I want you to have it. Honey, I don't have a lot of time left. I'd rather know that it's going to somebody who will love it and care for it than have it fall by the wayside, lost and forgotten. I think your mother would be happy to know you have it."

"Thank you, Miss Sandra."

"Now, tell me what you've been up to, and how you ended up back in Shiloh Springs."

BUCKLED INTO THE seat of the private plane Maggie chartered for Liam and Ruby's trip to Florida, Liam turned the box over and over in his hands. It was indeed a beautiful thing, though he knew it was probably common in its country of origin.

"Do you think that's the ring Uncle Piotr is desperately searching for?"

"Without a doubt." Liam opened the box and took it out, holding it up to the light and turning it this way and that.

"Any idea why it's so important? I understand it's got the family crest on it, but there must be more to it than that. He could have had another family ring made if it is that important."

Liam brushed his finger against the crest, wondering if it twisted off. Nope, nothing moved or shifted. He rubbed the scrollwork on the sides of the ruby but saw nothing out of the ordinary. The deep red color reminded him of blood. He wondered how much blood had been spilled in the hunt for this piece of jewelry?

"Can I see it?" Ruby held out her hand, and Liam dropped the ring onto her palm. She wrinkled her nose in the cutest way as she studied the ring. Suddenly, she started digging into her purse, a small clutch that she'd carried onto the plane. He'd been surprised because the women he knew carried more oversized bags containing everything but the kitchen sink. How could they find anything in those? It was like searching in the Bermuda Triangle whenever he'd been forced to look inside one.

"Ah-ha!" She pulled out a small pair of nail clippers and swiveled the tiny file out. Utilizing the sharp point, she dug it between the side of the ring and the ruby and wiggled it. At first, nothing happened, then suddenly the stone popped free. She wriggled her fingernail inside the opening and came out with a tiny circle.

"What's that?"

She grinned, her face lit up with excitement. "This, my friend, is what's known as a microdot. It's an old-fashioned way of compressing and hiding information. While it is an outdated model, it's possible that this," she pointed to the speck on her fingertip," is what my Uncle Piotr is looking for."

Liam stared at the tiny thing. Could this really be what everybody was hunting for? What kind of information was so important that people had died trying to retrieve it? This hidden gem had been the root cause of his Ruby having to fake her death and be out of his life for ten long years.

"What do you want to do with it?" He knew the decision had to be hers. She'd been the one to have her entire life turned inside out. As much as her decisions had affected him, he'd still had his family there to help him. Ruby had nobody. She'd lost everything, and this was one thing where she finally had control over.

"If I give it to Uncle Piotr, will he stop hounding me? I don't know, but I can't trust that he would. If I destroy it, that solves nothing. We don't know what's on this. What if revealing the information on here could change the world as we know it? Is it something we dare?"

Sliding his arm around her shoulder, he whispered in her ear. "I'll support you, no matter what you decide. I love you. I trust you."

Her breath caught, and she stared up at him. "You love me?"

"I never stopped loving you. I mourned you. I tried to move on when you were gone, but I couldn't because my heart always belonged to you, Ruby. Whether you feel the same or not doesn't change anything. I will be yours until the day I leave this earth, and I'll be waiting for you on the other side."

"I love you, too. I never stopped. I dreamt about you every night because you were the one constant, the one thing that kept me from going crazy. Nothing in my life was the same. I had nobody, nothing to lean on, except memories of you. I couldn't be with you, but nothing could make me stop loving you."

Liam's lips swooped down and covered hers, his lips devouring hers in a soul-searing kiss. He poured everything he felt into that kiss, wanting her to know without words how much he'd missed her. He wanted her to feel the truth of his love. When her lips parted beneath his, he deepened the kiss and felt her response. Nothing felt as right as kissing Ruby. His soul finally felt whole again, like half had been missing and now had found its mate.

Ruby finally pulled back, gasping for breath, and let out a breathy chuckle. "Wow."

"Wow, indeed. We always were combustible."

She leaned her head against his shoulder and sighed. "I know what I want to do with this." She lifted the microdot and looked at it again before carefully placing it back into the ring cavity. Replacing the stone, it looked exactly like it had before they'd found its buried treasure.

"Your decision. I'll back you, no matter what."

"I want to give it to Gage. Let him take it to the CIA. After that, what happens is out of our hands. Though to be honest, I hope they can nail Piotr to the wall for what he did to my mom. He needs to pay for stealing her life."

Liam leaned forward and placed a soft kiss against her forehead, being careful of the bump. Though it was smaller, it was still there. "I think you've made the right decision."

"Can you call Gage? Let him know what we found. I want this out of my possession as soon as possible."

"I can handle that. Gage and I decided to call a truce. I think he's doing it more for Momma, but I'll be good as long as he stops flirting with you."

Ruby rolled her eyes at his claim. "How many times do I have to tell you, there's nothing between Gage and me except friendship? Even that's questionable since I was a job for him. He was just like everybody else, wanting the information in this." She held up the ring, watching the blood-red ruby wink in the light.

Liam grinned when an idea popped into his head. It was a wicked, fantastic idea. His mother would probably kill him, but she'd get over it.

"You said you love me, Ruby mine?"

"Yes."

"Enough to marry me?"

Ruby's eyes widened at his question before she grinned and threw herself into his arms. "Yes, of course, I'll marry you!"

"Today?"

Would she go for it? He didn't want to wait another minute to make Ruby his wife. They'd already lost ten years. He didn't want to waste any more time.

"Wait. You want to get married today? How? I mean— can we do that?" He watched her nibble on her luscious bottom lip, and he pulled it free with his fingertip.

"All it would take is me walking to the cockpit and asking the pilot to take us to Vegas. We can have a big wedding later, with all the hoopla if you want, but I want to make you my wife today. As soon as we can legally stand before a preacher."

She giggled. "Your momma is gonna kill us."

"Is that a yes?" He held his breath, waiting for her answer.

"That's a yes!"

"Yeehaw!" He reached and unclipped her seatbelt, pulled her onto his lap, and kissed her with everything he had to give. Today would be the start of the second half of his life. The better half because he'd share it with Ruby.

"What about getting the ring to Gage?"

"We'll call him from Las Vegas. He wants it, he can come and pick it up. I'm sure the CIA will get him the fastest flight out there. But he'd better know we aren't turning this over to anybody but him." He touched the ring before picking up her purse and sliding the ring inside.

"Are we crazy?"

"If we are, then I don't ever want to be sane. You and me, Ruby mine. Forever."

"Well, if that's the case, handsome, you'd better tell the pilot we've got a wedding to get to."

CHAPTER TWENTY-FOUR
EPILOGUE

One week later

BRIAN LEANED AGAINST the wall in the back of the church rectory. He'd gotten out of the hospital a couple of days ago and still had to wear a sling on his arm to help immobilize the shoulder. Now that he'd been discharged, Brian refused the pain medication the surgeon prescribed, not taking anything stronger than ibuprofen. He needed to remain sharp and focused, not let narcotics dull his wits. That path led to destruction.

Liam and Ruby held center stage at this party, an impromptu wedding reception. The newlywed couple had eloped to Las Vegas the week before, getting married without fanfare or the usual trappings that accompanied big family weddings.

Glancing toward Ms. Patti, Brian wondered how she'd taken the news about her son slipping away with his love to get married without telling anyone. Outwardly she'd taken the news with her usual aplomb but secretly he knew she'd been hurt and disappointed. He had a feeling that for Ms.

Patti, watching her children pledge their life and their love to their chosen partner was the culmination of a journey that started from the moment each son arrived at the Boudreau ranch.

Liam wouldn't have deliberately hurt his mother in any way, Brian was sure of that. He'd simply gotten a spur-of-the-moment idea and ran with it. Ruby undoubtedly encouraged him. Not that he blamed either one. They'd lost more than enough of their lives to deception, lies, and threats. Moving forward was the best choice they could make, and he was happy for them.

"Why are you standing over here all by your lonesome?" Rafe held two bottles in his hands, one a longneck beer and the other a Dr Pepper. Lifting both, he smiled as he handed the soda to Brian.

"Wondering why I'm even here in the first place if I'm being honest." Brian took a long swallow of the icy cold drink.

"I'd think that was obvious. You were invited. From what I heard, not only did Momma call you with a personal invitation, Liam and Ruby asked you to come."

"This is a family gathering. I shouldn't be here."

Rafe barked out a laugh and moved to stand beside Brian, his back against the wall. "If you haven't realized it yet, buddy, you are family. After everything you've done, helping out Boudreaus in one way or another, you'd be an official member of the family in everything but name. Of course, you have the option of changing that, too, if you want. Becoming a legal Boudreau is kind of a family tradition. But you're a special case. Notice I didn't say a hard case, though that applies. You've carved out your special place in Momma's heart between you living at the Big House when you were a kid and what you did recently. Dad's too, if we're being honest. When you showed back up in Shiloh Springs, your fate was sealed."

Brian swallowed past the sudden lump in his throat. "How is Douglas? I'd planned to drop by the hospital before all this," Brian gestured toward his sling, "happened."

"Dad's doing better. Fortunately, he's healthy for the most part. I think this episode might have thrown a scare into him, and he will take better care of himself. Momma's gonna make sure of that."

"That's good. If he needs anything…"

"He's good. His heart is in great shape, according to Doc Shaw. No stroke, though his blood pressure was sky high when they admitted him. He's lucky that's all it was. Now he's on medication to help control it, and Liam will take over more responsibility at the company. I doubt Dad will ever fully retire, but Momma's convinced him to take some time off. She wants him to slow down a bit. Spend some time with her. Maybe do a little traveling or something."

Brian tried to picture Douglas Boudreau slowing down and couldn't manage it. The man was larger-than-life and always on the go. Of course, Ms. Patti was just as bad.

Maybe worse. The petite woman didn't seem to have an off switch. He couldn't remember a time when she wasn't neck-deep in everything going on in Shiloh Springs. Yet she'd always had time for a gangly, awkward kid who didn't seem to fit in anywhere.

A burst of laughter came from the happy couple, and everyone's attention shifted to them, and the three-tier white and silver wedding cake Jill had provided for the reception. Brian admitted he didn't know much about baked goods and the artistry behind making them, other than he liked eating them. But the cake she'd provided was a thing of beauty.

"Bet she smashes that bite of cake in his face." Rafe nodded to where Ruby stood with a piece of cake in her hand. Liam took a step back as she advanced, her grin mischievous.

"I think Liam might have the same idea."

When Liam and Ruby both smeared cake over each other's faces, Brian smiled. It was nice to see somebody get the happily ever after they deserved. Far too often, people got together for reasons other than love and ended up bitter and hurt, angry and vindictive. Yet, somehow, the Boudreaus seemed to have the magic touch. Each one of them seemed to find their perfect match.

Findings his true match wasn't in the cards, though. With his life, the kind of cases he worked, asking anyone to deal with that wasn't right or fair. Maybe he could be the honorary uncle to some Boudreau young'uns when they had them. He'd show up on birthdays and holidays, load 'em up with presents and enough sugar for their parents to blow a gasket, and then head back to his lonely apartment. Yep, that sounded about right.

Spotting Ms. Patti across the room, he decided now might be a good time to call it a night. If his boss hadn't ordered him to take at least two weeks off, he'd already be back at work. The case he'd been working on wasn't going to solve itself. He wished it would because this was one of those slow grind cases, mostly watching paint dry kind of cases, where nothing happened for weeks on end. Sometimes sitting back and surveilling suspects was the most challenging part of his job. However, it did leave him with a lot of time on his hands. Time he'd used to keep tabs on all the Boudreaus.

It turned out that his former foster brothers led fascinating lives. Who'd have thought it?

Ms. Patti smiled when he moved closer, holding open her arms for a hug. She was one of the most touchy-feely people he'd ever met, though he couldn't help wondering if she was that way with everybody or only a select group. It didn't matter, he was happy to be included in the ones she cared about.

"How are you holding up? The shoulder bothering you?"

"Everything's good. I thought I'd call it a day. I've got a bit of a drive in the morning and thought I'd turn in early."

"Oh, that's a shame. I was hoping you could stick around Shiloh Springs for a couple more days." She gently patted the arm that wasn't in the sling. "You work too hard."

"If I don't, who'd catch the bad guys?"

Her lips twitched at his pun. "You seem to have a knack for finding the most elusive baddies, don't you?"

"Just call me a trouble magnet, Ms. Patti."

The moment the words left his mouth, he caught sight of long blonde ringlets with hints of cotton-candy pink peeking through. The curls caressed bared shoulders and a body encased in a royal blue dress molded to delicious curves. Even seeing her from the back, she fit the kind of woman he was attracted to. He almost wished she'd turn around so he could see her face. His heartbeat skipped a beat before adrenaline raced through his body. Who was she?

Ms. Patti must have noticed his distracted stare and tracked his gaze to the mystery woman. She gently touched his arm again.

"That's Harper Westbrook. She's a friend of Jill's. They used to work together. Would you like to meet her?"

He started to decline her offer because now wasn't a good time to get involved. Especially with somebody from Shiloh Springs, because he wasn't about to fool around where his friends lived. That was asking for trouble—trouble he didn't need.

When Harper turned around, the bottom fell out of Brian's world. Because he recognized her face. It was the face that had haunted his dreams for months, the gorgeous heart-shape with arched brows above the prettiest green eyes he'd ever seen. Disappointment and regret rode him, because this night had just gone from a friendly gathering with family to an extension of his FBI case.

Harper Westbrook, Jill's friend, was a wanted criminal, involved in the case he'd been working on for months. He knew her face, but he hadn't known her name until tonight.

Could this night possibly get any worse? Guess it could, he thought, because he was going to have to cause a scene.

He needed to arrest Harper Westbrook.

For murder.

Thank you for reading Liam, Book #11 in the Texas Boudreau Brotherhood series. I hope you enjoyed Liam and Ruby's story. Want to find out more about *Brian McKenna and the excitement and adventure he's about to plunge headfirst into*? Brian is one of Ms. Patti's "Lost Boys", and he keeps turning up in Shiloh Springs every time there's something exciting happening. But he's about to meet his match in Harper Westbrook.

Go to the preorder link below to order your copy of, *Brian, Book #12 in the Texas Boudreau Brotherhood. Available at all major e-book and print vendors.*

www.kathyivan.com/Brian.html

NEWSLETTER SIGN UP

Don't want to miss out on any new books, contests, and free stuff? Sign up to get my newsletter. I promise not to spam you, and only send out notifications/e-mails whenever there's a new release or contest/giveaway. Follow the link and join today!

http://eepurl.com/baqdRX

REVIEWS ARE IMPORTANT!

People are always asking how they can help spread the word about my books. One of the best ways to do that is by word of mouth. Tell your friends about the books and recommend them. Share them on Goodreads. If you find a book or series or author you love – talk about it. Everybody loves to find out about new books and new-to-them authors, especially if somebody they know has read the book and loved it.

The next best thing is to write a review. Writing a review for a book does not have to be long or detailed. It can be as simple as saying "I loved the book."

I hope you enjoyed reading Liam, Texas Boudreau Brotherhood.

If you liked the story, I hope you'll consider leaving a review for the book at the vendor where you purchased it and at Goodreads. Reviews are the best way to spread the word to others looking for good books. It truly helps.

BOOKS BY KATHY IVAN

www.kathyivan.com/books.html

TEXAS BOUDREAU BROTHERHOOD

Rafe

Antonio

Brody

Ridge

Lucas

Heath

Shiloh

Chance

Derrick

Dane

Liam

Brian (coming soon)

Texas Boudreau Brotherhood Series Box Set Books 1-3

NEW ORLEANS CONNECTION SERIES

Desperate Choices

Connor's Gamble

Relentless Pursuit

Ultimate Betrayal

Keeping Secrets

Sex, Lies and Apple Pies

Deadly Justice

Wicked Obsession

Hidden Agenda

Spies Like Us

Fatal Intentions

New Orleans Connection Series Box Set: Books 1-3

New Orleans Connection Series Box Set: Books 4-7

CAJUN CONNECTION SERIES

Saving Sarah

Saving Savannah

Saving Stephanie

Guarding Gabi

LOVIN' LAS VEGAS SERIES

It Happened In Vegas

Crazy Vegas Love

Marriage, Vegas Style

A Virgin In Vegas

Vegas, Baby!

Yours For The Holidays

Match Made In Vegas

One Night In Vegas

Last Chance In Vegas

Lovin' Las Vegas (box set books 1-3)

OTHER BOOKS BY KATHY IVAN

Second Chances (Destiny's Desire Book #1)

ABOUT THE AUTHOR

USA TODAY Bestselling author Kathy Ivan spent most of her life with her nose between the pages of a book. It didn't matter if the book was a paranormal romance, romantic suspense, action and adventure thrillers, sweet & spicy, or a sexy novella. Kathy turned her obsession with reading into the next logical step, writing.

Her books transport you to the sultry splendor of the French Quarter in New Orleans in her award-winning romantic suspense, or to Las Vegas in her contemporary romantic comedies. Kathy's new romantic suspense series features, Texas Boudreau Brotherhood, features alpha heroes in small town Texas. Gotta love those cowboys!

Kathy tells stories people can't get enough of; reuniting old loves, betrayal of trust, finding kidnapped children, psychics and sometimes even a ghost or two. But one thing they all have in common – love and a happily ever after). More about Kathy and her books can be found at

WEBSITE: www.kathyivan.com

Follow Kathy on Facebook at facebook.com/kathyivanauthor

Follow Kathy on Twitter at twitter.com/@kathyivan

Follow Kathy at BookBub
bookbub.com/profile/kathy-ivan

DISCARD

CPSIA information can be obtained
at www.ICGtesting.com
Printed in the USA
LVHW020619270722
724372LV00013B/370